GANSETT ISLAND EPISODES

EPISODE 1: VICTORIA & SHANNON

MARIE FORCE

Published by HTJB, Inc.
Copyright 2017. HTJB, Inc.
Cover designer: Kristina Brinton
Interior Layout: Isabel Sullivan, E-book Formatting Fairies

ISBN: 978-1946136107

www.marieforce.com

The Gansett Island Series

Book 1: Maid for Love

Book 2: Fool for Love

Book 3: Ready for Love

Book 4: Falling for Love

Book 5: Hoping for Love

Book 6: Season for Love

Book 7: Longing for Love

Book 8: Waiting for Love

Book 9: Time for Love

Book 10: Meant for Love

Book 10.5: Chance for Love,

A Gansett Island Novella

Book 11: Gansett After Dark

Book 12: Kisses After Dark

Book 13: Love After Dark

Book 14: Celebration After Dark

Book 15: Desire After Dark

Book 16: Light After Dark

Gansett Island Episodes, Episode 1: Victoria & Shannon

CHAPTER 1

Desperate times called for desperate measures, or that was what Victoria Stevens told herself as she took an early lunch break for an errand she'd put off long enough. She had tried everything she could think of to get her boyfriend, Shannon, to open up to her without success, and there was only one person on this island who could help her figure out what to do next.

On paper, Victoria was one half of a perfect relationship. Together nearly a year, she and Shannon O'Grady enjoyed a lot of the same activities, TV shows and friends. They'd lived together for almost a year, laughed often, hardly fought and had the hottest sex she'd ever had with anyone almost every day. Though she told herself it couldn't be better, that was a big, fat lie. It could be better. It could be a *lot* better.

What they had, she'd finally been forced to acknowledge, was a lovely, wonderful surface relationship that lacked the kind of true intimacy she craved. She saw what she wanted for herself every day in the couples she worked with as a Certified Nurse Midwife, and refused to settle for less in her own life. So even if her relationship with Shannon seemed perfect on the surface, the foundation was shaky.

For one thing, they never talked about anything important beyond their work schedules, what was for dinner or whether they should go to a party they'd been invited to. In some ways, she felt like she didn't know him any better now than she had the day she met him, and that was a problem she couldn't continue to ignore as much as she might want to.

Five years ago, she would've ignored it. She would've told herself to stop being melodramatic and enjoy what she had. The future would take care of itself. But staring down her twenty-ninth birthday had her taking stock of where she'd expected to be by thirty—and it was *not* in a go-nowhere relationship with the hottest guy she'd ever met, let alone dated.

She'd waited until Shannon, a deckhand for the Gansett Island Ferry Company, departed on the eleven o'clock boat to the mainland. As she walked into town from the clinic where she worked, she saw the boat he was on way off in the distance. That meant the coast was clear for her trip to the ferry landing, which bustled with activity on a Friday in late June.

This was the right thing to do, or so she told herself. If she allowed in any other thought, such as the propriety of asking Shannon's cousin questions she probably ought to ask Shannon himself, she might chicken out, and that was not an option. Outside the door to the ferry company's main office, she took a deep breath and knocked on Seamus O'Grady's open door.

He was on the phone and waved her in.

Victoria went into his office and took one of the chairs that sat in front of his desk.

"I understand," he said in the lyrical Irish accent that was so familiar to her after a year with his cousin. "I appreciate the call. I'll have a talk with him tonight and get back to you tomorrow. Very good. Thank you." Sighing, he ended the call and placed his cell phone on the desk. "Sorry about that."

"Everything okay?"

"Jackson is having a few challenges at summer camp," Seamus said of one of the two brothers he and his wife, Carolina, had taken in after their mother died of lung cancer. "Getting into some scrapes with the other kids and 'acting out,' or so the director says. I'll admit to being out of my league with things like this."

"You're doing great, and you'll figure out what to do."

"I hope you're right, but you didn't come by to talk about my woes, did you?"

"No," she said with a smile, "I came to talk about *my* woes."

His brows knitted with concern. "What's wrong?"

"Shannon."

"What about him? I thought things were going great for the two of you."

"Things *are* great." Victoria paused and shook her head. "No, that's not true. It *could* be great, but it's like there's this gigantic brick wall standing between us, and I can't get around it or over it or through it no matter how hard I try."

"Ahhh," Seamus said, nodding. "I see."

"I hope you know... I'd never bother you with this if I wasn't feeling sort of desperate about what to do."

"First of all, love, you're never a bother. We're friends, aren't we?"

"I'd like to think so." She and Shannon spent a lot of time with Seamus and Carolina and now their boys, too. The four of them regularly went out to dinner, played cards and spent holidays together.

He stood. "Take a walk with me. This isn't a short conversation."

Victoria got up to go with him, eager to hear what he had to say even if part of her was afraid, too.

They walked to the pier where the fishing boats came and went, bringing in fresh catch-of-the-day that was sold to island residents and restaurants. In the middle of the day, the pier was mostly deserted, with many of the boats out on the water.

"Has he told you about Fiona?" Seamus asked after a long silence.

"Who?" Victoria immediately thought of the woman who worked with Grace McCarthy at the pharmacy, but clearly Seamus meant someone else.

"I didn't think so."

"Who is she?"

"She was his first love back in Ireland." He rested his arms on one of the pilings and stared out at the ocean. "It's still hard to talk about her even after all these years."

Suddenly, Victoria was sorry she'd sought him out and particularly sorry she'd asked questions she had no business asking. "I, um, maybe it would be better if I didn't know."

"Would it?"

He was giving her an out, and Victoria wanted to take it because she sensed that whatever he was about to tell her would change everything. Was that what she wanted? To change everything? "I... I don't know."

"You want to understand him, right?"

She nodded.

"Then you need to know about Fiona."

Resigned to hearing the story, Victoria leaned against the next piling, needing the support it provided.

"I can't remember a time when they weren't together. They met in school and were inseparable from then on. After they finished school, they moved to Dublin so she could pursue a career as a model. Shannon got a job as a bartender to help make ends meet so she could focus on her career, which was really taking off. She had a top agent and a couple of photographers who loved to work with her."

Victoria wanted to run away from whatever was coming next. "Wh-What happened?"

"I'm only going to tell you this much, love. She was murdered."

Victoria felt like she'd been punched. "Oh God," she whispered.

"I'll leave it to him to share the details, if he chooses to. I've already said more than I should have. He's intensely private on this topic. He doesn't talk about her at all."

Her heart ached for Shannon. Tears flooded her eyes, spilling down her cheeks.

"As you can imagine, he's never been the same since she died. For a long time afterward, we worried he'd take his own life rather than have to live without her. So we made sure someone was always with him the first year. We watched him around the clock. The second year, he started drinking and spent most of that year and the next drunk. By the time he finally snapped out of that stage, we were about to send him to rehab. But one day, he got up, took a shower, got dressed and went back to work at the bar, as if nothing had happened. That's what he did for years—got up, went to work, did what he had to do to survive. Then, eight years after he lost Fiona, he came here and met you, and he's been different."

"How so?" she asked, her voice scratchy. "How has he been different?"

"He smiles again. He laughs. He participates. You have no idea what a huge improvement those things are from the way he was for so long."

Using her sleeve, she tried to mop up the tears. "I've wondered," she said haltingly, "why it seemed he was willing to go only so far with me. Now I know it's because he isn't capable of more."

"A year ago, I would've agreed with you. Now, I'm not so sure that's true."

"Why do you say that?"

"I've spent a lot of time with the two of you. I've seen the way he looks at you and watches you when you're in the room, looks for you when you're not. He's as invested in you as he's able to be, even if he doesn't say so."

"I'm not sure what to do with this information, Seamus." She'd gotten way more than she'd bargained for from Shannon's cousin.

"What do you want to do with it?" he asked.

"I want to find him and hold him and tell him I love him and I always will even if he's not capable of loving me back."

"He's capable. He just doesn't know it yet. You'll have to lead him to it if you're interested in a future with him. Is that what you want, Vic? A future with him?"

"I think so," she said softly. "But I can't compete with her. I feel awful even saying that."

"I understand, and you shouldn't feel awful. For what it's worth, I see the way he is with you, and I think he cares for you more than either of you realize."

"Do I tell him what I know?"

"That's up to you, love. I can't tell you how to play this. I wish I could."

"Will he mind that you told me?"

"If he does, that's between the two of us. Don't you worry about me. I can fight my own battles. I told you what I did because I like you for him. I like you two together, and I wanted to help. My intentions were pure, and that's what I'll tell him if it comes to that."

"I really appreciate this, Seamus."

He held out his arms to her, and she walked willingly into his embrace. "He's lucky to have you in his life, and he knows it. Have some faith in that."

"I'll try," she said, smiling up at him. "Your wife is lucky to have you, too."

"Aye, I tell her so every day."

Victoria laughed at the predictable comment. "I'll see you later." She walked back to the clinic lost in thought and grief-stricken over what Shannon had been through losing his first love in such a horrific way. So many things made sense to her now that she knew what'd happened to him.

Most of the time, he came off as a happy-go-lucky sort of guy. However, every so often, the darkness would swoop in, and he'd punch out of their relationship for a day or two, even if he never physically left the home they shared. Victoria had learned to give him space during the dark moods, even as she wondered what caused them. Now she knew, and understood, for the most part anyway. If only she could figure out how best to use the information Seamus had given her to improve their relationship.

In her heart of hearts, she believed they had what it took to make this the kind of love story that lasted a lifetime. But that could happen only if they both wanted it. She couldn't do it on her own. She was still pondering her predicament when she walked through the main doors to the clinic. Dr. David Lawrence stood at the registration desk, speaking with Katie Lawry, their nurse practitioner, and Anna, the receptionist.

"Oh, there you are," David said. "I was about to call you."

"Why? What's up?"

"Tiffany Taylor is in labor in Exam Three." He took a closer look at her. "Have you been crying?"

She shook her head. "No."

"Vic… What's wrong?"

"Let's talk about it later." As her colleagues looked at her with concern, Victoria took Tiffany's chart from David and went through the double doors to the exam rooms, knocking on the door to number three. "Hi there," she said to Tiffany, owner of the Naughty & Nice boutique, and her husband, Blaine, the island's police chief. "What's this I hear about labor?"

"We were in bed, and she woke up in a puddle," Blaine said, seeming incredibly stressed.

"Any contractions?"

"Over the last day or two, I've had like a rolling ache that comes and goes pretty regularly, but since it didn't feel like the labor pains I had with Ashleigh, I thought they were Braxton-Hicks contractions. Not the real thing."

"Let's take a look." Victoria washed her hands and put on gloves before helping Tiffany into position. As this was Tiff's second child, she knew the drill.

Victoria performed an internal exam and discovered Tiffany was fully dilated and effaced. "You work fast, Mrs. Taylor. You're about to have this baby."

"Right now?" Blaine asked, sounding panicked. "She's not due for another week. This was supposed to happen on the mainland."

"Well, it's happening right here and now."

"What if something goes wrong or she needs a C-section?"

"We have everything we need if that should happen." After David had delivered his ex-fiancée Janey Cantrell's baby by emergency C-section last year, they'd taken steps to bring in the proper equipment to perform emergency surgery, if necessary. They never again wanted to be unprepared for an emergency of that magnitude. "The best thing you both can do is relax and breathe. Tiffany had an easy labor with Ashleigh, and there's no reason to believe this one won't be routine, too."

As she said the words, Tiffany's face tightened with obvious pain. "I'm feeling the need to push." She clung to Blaine's hand. "Can I push?"

"Not quite yet. Let me get everything ready, and then we'll get that baby out." She left the exam room to round up help.

"What's going on?" Katie asked.

"She's ready to deliver now, and I think it's going to be quick. Can you give me a hand?"

"I'm all yours in five minutes. I've got to move a few things around."

"Ask Anna to clear my afternoon, will you?" In Victoria's world, nothing took precedence over a mom in labor.

"You got it." Katie went to speak to the receptionist.

"You're sure you're all right?" David asked when they met up in the hallway.

"Can we talk after work? I've got a baby to deliver."

"Of course."

"Thanks." David was one of her closest friends, and there was no one else she'd rather talk to about what she should do with the information Seamus had given her.

Victoria put her long dark hair up in a bun, donned a gown and thoroughly washed her hands. Right now she needed to focus on the new life that Tiffany was about to bring into the world. She'd have plenty of time later to figure out what she was going to do about her own life.

CHAPTER 2

Victoria used the sleeve of her gown to wipe sweat from her brow. "Come on, Tiffany. One more big push."

"I can't," Tiffany said, weeping.

"Yes, you can, babe," Blaine said, cheering her on as he had for two hours now.

It was taking longer than Victoria had thought it would to get the baby out. She was keeping a close eye on the baby's heart rate and Tiffany's vital signs. So far they were both hanging in there, but she was anxious to see the baby safely delivered.

"Why's it taking so long?" Tiffany asked. "I had Ash in thirty minutes. Aren't second babies supposed to come faster?"

"They're all different," Victoria said, eyeing the monitor. "Here comes another contraction."

Tiffany pushed as hard as she could, but the baby was obstinate.

"We're almost there." Victoria tried to stay cheerful and upbeat during deliveries, hoping the moms would take strength from her positive attitude. "Rest for a minute, and then we'll do it again."

Blaine sat behind Tiffany on the delivery table, his arms around her, and spoke softly to her between contractions as he wiped her tears with a tissue and her face with the cool cloths that Katie handed him after every contraction.

A knock on the door sent Katie to find out what was up. She came back with an odd expression on her face. "Jenny Martinez is here. She might also be in labor."

"You've got to be kidding me," Victoria said.

"Wish I was. David is with her for now."

Didn't it figure that all hell would break loose on a day when she wanted nothing more than to go home and be with Shannon?

Tiffany's sister, Maddie McCarthy, came to the door, looking frantic and overheated, which wasn't recommended due to her own pregnancy. "I came as soon as we got back from the mainland," Maddie said.

"Come in," Tiffany said, holding out a hand to her sister, who rushed to Tiffany's bedside to hug her.

"How're you doing?" Maddie asked.

"Terrible. The baby won't come out."

"She's doing great," Victoria said. "Her little one has a mind of his or her own."

"Just like his or her mom," Blaine said, drawing a small smile from his wife.

Victoria eyed the monitor and noted the start of another contraction. "Let's do it again, Tiffany."

"Come on, sweetheart," Blaine said, his arms around her as he supported her from behind. "You got this. I can't wait to meet our baby."

With Maddie holding her hand and offering added encouragement, Tiffany pushed harder than she had in a while.

Victoria watched as the baby crowned. "That's it. Don't stop now, Tiff. You're almost there."

Tiffany screamed from the effort it took to keep pushing.

Victoria delivered the baby's head and then the shoulders. "One more good push." And with that, the baby slid into Victoria's waiting hands. Holding the squalling infant, she stood to show her off to her exhausted parents. "You have a little girl. Congratulations! Dad, do you want to cut the cord?"

"I'll let you take care of that," Blaine said, wiping tears from his own face as well as Tiffany's.

Victoria took care of the cord and handed the baby to Katie to be cleaned up before she got to officially meet her parents. Victoria delivered the placenta and determined that Tiffany needed a few stitches to deal with some tearing. She worked through the post-delivery steps one after the other with single-minded focus on her patient.

David evaluated the baby and declared her perfectly healthy. He wrapped her in a receiving blanket and brought her to meet her overjoyed parents.

"Oh my goodness," Blaine said on a long exhale. "Will you *look* at that face?"

"Another girl who looks just like her mother," Maddie said.

"Three of them will be the death of me," Blaine replied as he contended with a new flood of tears.

"Hi, baby," Tiffany said, running her finger over her daughter's cheek.

"What's her name?" Victoria asked.

"Adeline Francine Taylor," Tiffany said. "Adeline is Blaine's grandmother's name, and Francine for my mom."

"That's beautiful," Maddie said. "I love it, and Mom will be thrilled. Do you want me to call her?"

"Yes, please. Everything happened so fast that I never got around to calling anyone. How did you hear?"

"Katie told Shane." Katie's fiancé, Shane, and Maddie's husband, Mac, were cousins. "He called Mac. We got back on the first ferry that had room for the car."

"I feel bad that your trip got cut short."

On Victoria's recommendation, Maddie and Mac had gone to the mainland to consult with the specialist at Women & Infants in Providence. After her last pregnancy ended in miscarriage, they were leaving nothing to chance.

"Only by a day that we were going to spend at the beach," Maddie said. "Nothing to worry about."

"And everything is okay?" Tiffany asked.

"So far so good. It's the waiting that's the hard part."

"You're already past the point you were when you lost Connor."

"I know." Maddie smiled at her sister. "No talk of sad things today. This is baby Adeline's day. Let me call Mom to get her, Ned and Ashleigh over here to meet their new granddaughter and sister."

"Thanks, Maddie."

"I'm going to check on another patient," Victoria said. "I'll be back to look in on you guys shortly."

"Thanks for everything, Vic," Tiffany said. "I never could've gotten through this pregnancy and delivery without your support."

"I'm so happy for you all." Victoria left them with a smile, removed her gown and tossed it into a hamper. Then she went into her office to send a quick text to Shannon. *Outbreak of babies around here today. I'll be late.*

He responded right away. *No bother, love. I'll keep dinner warm for you.*

Don't worry about dinner for me. Will grab something here.

Okay, see you when you get home.

Every time she helped bring a new life into the world, she wondered if she'd ever get to share that experience with a man she loved above all others. Seeing Blaine and Tiffany with their newborn baby made Victoria yearn for a child of her own with the man she loved. Interestingly enough, she'd never had such yearnings until she met Shannon O'Grady.

She took a deep cleansing breath, the kind she encouraged her laboring moms to take, and left her office to see to Jenny Martinez, a first-time mom at age thirty-eight. Victoria had kept a close eye on Jenny, especially during the last few weeks. Like Tiffany, Jenny had planned to deliver on the mainland, but her baby apparently had other plans.

Victoria couldn't wait to see what these strong-willed babies would be like as two-year-olds.

"Hi there," she said to Jenny and her husband, Alex, when she entered the room where Jenny was hooked to monitors. Alex stood next to the bed holding her hand, looking as stressed as Blaine had earlier. "How're you doing?"

"Not so great," Jenny said. "The pain is pretty bad. Worse than advertised."

"I wish I had a dollar for every time I've heard that from a first-time mom in labor," Victoria said. "Let's take a look." During the internal exam, Victoria determined that Jenny was fully effaced but only seven centimeters dilated. "You've got a little ways to go before you'll be ready to deliver."

Jenny groaned at that news. "How little of a ways?"

"Three more centimeters, but you're doing great."

"We hadn't planned to have the baby on the island," Alex said, looking a little wild around the eyes. "Are you sure it'll be safe?"

"We'll do everything we can to make sure it's perfectly safe," Victoria assured him. "As we've talked about over the last few weeks, there's always a possibility of complications. I don't expect any problems, but if we encounter something we can't handle, we can have a chopper here within minutes and get you to Providence. Okay?"

Alex nodded in agreement, but she could tell he was only partially pacified by her answer.

She didn't blame him for being concerned. Island deliveries were never recommended, but they happened. Not usually two in one day, but Victoria delivered, on average, about six babies a year in the clinic. She'd delivered Laura Lawry's twins in March when they arrived early. In her line of work, best-laid plans often went awry.

"What're you thinking about pain meds?" Victoria asked Jenny.

She glanced at Alex and then said, "I'm going to try to go without."

"Are you sure? If we wait much longer, it'll be too late."

"I think I'm sure."

"Babe, if you need it, do it," Alex said. "Victoria wouldn't give you anything that would hurt the baby."

"I know, but I really want to be drug-free."

"Then that's what we'll do," Victoria said, patting Jenny's knee. "I'll be back to check on you in a little while."

"Thanks, Vic."

David met her in the hallway. "You need food."

"I'm okay."

"Could be a long night. I'll order from Mario's. You want your usual?"

She wasn't sure she could eat, but she nodded anyway. "Sure, that'd be great."

"Coming right up. Go take five while you can. I'll find you when the food gets here, and I'll keep an eye on everyone in the meantime."

"Thanks, David."

"No problem."

Victoria went into her office, took her hair down from the bun and stretched out on the sofa she'd bought at a yard sale for occasions such as this when she was required to stay at the clinic after hours. Rarely did she have to spend an entire night, but it happened once in a while. In a way, she was thankful for the outbreak of babies, because it bought her some time to figure out her next move with Shannon.

Looking up at the ceiling, she thought about the night she'd met him at the Beachcomber, the same day he'd arrived from Ireland with his aunt Nora, Seamus's mother. He'd planned to stay for two weeks and go home with Nora. Victoria wasn't particularly proud of the fact that she'd invited him back to her place the first night they met. That wasn't something she'd ever done before him. But it had been a while, years really, since she'd connected with a man the way she had with him. And, let's face it. The man was smoking hot.

She smiled thinking about how bowled over she'd been by his charm, the accent and a face that defied description. He was male beauty personified, with longish brown hair infused with red highlights that went blond in the summer, hazel eyes, a body built for sin and lips made for kissing. To this day, when he spoke to her in that lyrical Irish accent, she went stupid in the head. He could be talking about taking out the trash, and it had the same impact as when he whispered sweet words when they made love.

Closing her eyes, she thought about that first time, when he'd silently helped her out of her clothes and then let her do the same for him. She'd been slightly appalled at how easily she'd capitulated to his overwhelming charm, but once they were in her bed, she hadn't had the mental capacity for regrets *or* recriminations.

She'd had the best sex of her entire life that night—and just about every night since then. It was safe to say she was completely addicted to sex with him. Just thinking about it made her want him. Closing her eyes, she allowed herself to indulge in thoughts about the part of their relationship that worked effortlessly. All he had to do was look at her, and she was ready. It had never been like that for her before with any guy, even Stuart, the man she'd dated for two years after college.

Marrying him would've been a huge mistake. What if she'd been married to him or someone else when she met Shannon? How would she have resisted the instant temptation he presented? She'd wanted him from the minute he sat next to her at the Beachcomber bar and asked for a beer. He had her at "I'll have a Guinness, please, love."

Even Chelsea, the bartender, had reacted the way any normal red-blooded American woman would in the face of so much Irish hotness. The "holy cow" look she'd given Victoria had been priceless. But Shannon… He'd had eyes only for her, something that still had the power to amaze her so many months later.

They'd had an intense two weeks, fueled by the time limit on his visit. She'd actually taken vacation days so they could spend more time together before he had to leave. Okay, truthfully, they'd spent all those vacation days in her bed, getting up only to shower and eat before going back for more. Then, when the time had come for Nora to depart, he'd asked Victoria if she'd like him to stay.

She'd cried from the relief of knowing she got to keep him—for now anyway. He'd moved into her place that day and had been there ever since, paying his half of the rent and other expenses by working as a mate on the ferries that were managed by his cousin. Seamus had secured a work visa for Shannon that allowed him to stay in the country. Since then, they'd fallen into a satisfying routine that consisted of spending every free minute together. She still couldn't get enough of him or the way she felt when she was with him.

But the longer they'd been together, the more she'd begun to wonder about what he *wasn't* telling her. The dark moods, his refusal to say much of anything about his life in Ireland and his seeming intention to keep things light rather than serious between them had driven her to seek some answers. She'd gone to Seamus wanting to know why Shannon seemed only capable of a satisfying domestic and sexual relationship but nothing more than that.

Now she knew, and after hearing what he'd endured, she wished she'd left well enough alone.

A knock on the door snapped her out of the introspection. She sat up and ran her hands through her hair. "Come in."

David poked his head in. "Food's here. Katie said for us to eat first, and then she will. Is it okay if we eat in here?"

"Sure."

He came in with the bag from Mario's and set up their dinner on the coffee table she'd bought at the island's weekly flea market.

She opened the fragrant container of pasta primavera and poured Italian dressing on the tossed salad. As usual, David had gotten chicken parmesan for himself. "I hope Jenny likes the aroma of garlic in her delivery room," Victoria said.

"She'll be too busy having a baby to notice. I just looked in on her, and she's doing okay. Tiffany is taking a nap while Blaine is with the baby. All is well."

"Thank you. What a crazy day."

"Good thing this doesn't happen very often."

"No kidding. Let's hope Sydney Harris behaves herself and doesn't go early, too."

"Don't even say it."

They ate in companionable silence for a few minutes. Then he glanced over at her. "Are you going tell me why you were crying when you came back from lunch?"

CHAPTER 3

Victoria wiped her mouth with one of the paper napkins Mario's had sent with their order and took a sip from the bottle of water David had gotten her. "I went to see Seamus."

"Okay…"

"I asked him about Shannon. I… I wanted to know why our relationship seems to be stuck in first gear. Not that first gear is bad. It's actually really nice, but…"

"You want it to be more."

"I was hoping it could be more. Eventually. Now…" Victoria shrugged. "It's probably not going to happen."

"Why do you say that? What did Seamus tell you?"

She sighed deeply. "He told me about Shannon's first love, Fiona, the woman he was with from childhood who was murdered."

"Oh my God. How?"

"Seamus said I'd have to let Shannon tell me the details, if he chooses to. He didn't want to go too far in filling in the blanks for me."

"And Shannon has never told you anything about her?"

Victoria shook her head. "I'd never heard her name before today."

"Oh wow."

"I don't know what to do with this info, David. Do I tell him I know about her or respect his obvious desire to never speak of her? Do I settle for the perfectly good thing we have now, or do I rock the boat and hope we can make it something even better?"

"That's a tough one, for sure. Would he be angry with Seamus for telling you?"

"Seamus says probably not, and if he is, they'll work that out between them."

After a long moment of quiet during which Victoria picked at her food while David wolfed his down with his usual enthusiasm for all things edible, he looked over at her. "It comes down to what *you* want. Mentioning this to him would be a risk. He might not appreciate questions about her from you. That could put a wedge between you, but it could also bring you closer. Maybe he's been trying to find the right time to tell you about her. There's really no way to predict which way it'll go. Are you prepared for the possibility that you knowing about her could make him angry?"

"No, I'm not prepared for that, and I'd never want to do anything to resurrect painful memories for him, but I feel like the ghost of his dead love is standing squarely in the middle of our relationship. We'll never be able to move forward until we confront her."

"And you're sure that's what you want? To move forward with him?"

"Yes. I want everything with him. I'm crazy about him. I have been from the very beginning."

"I know," he said with a smirk. "I was there and had to hear the gory details."

"There was nothing gory about those details."

"Depends on which side of the conversation you were on."

Victoria laughed. "I suppose that's true." She sighed again. "I'm so afraid of bringing this up with him. The last thing I want to do is hurt him."

"Maybe you could bring it up without mentioning her name. You could say, 'I understand that you have reasons for not wanting this to be more than it already is, but I was hoping we might talk about the future and where we might be heading.' That would give you a chance to tell him what you want and to hear what he thinks."

"Why does the thought of saying that make me feel sick?"

"Because you're scared of losing something that's come to mean a lot to you."

"I don't want to lose him," she said softly, blinking back tears that made her feel weak. Victoria Stevens, badass Certified Nurse Midwife and overall happy person, did not *cry* over men. At least she never had before, even when she broke up with Stuart before he could propose and force her to turn him down.

David put his arm around her, and Victoria rested her head on his shoulder.

"Thanks for letting me dump this on you."

"You can dump on me any time. That's what friends are for."

"I need to check on my patients."

"I've got Tiffany and the baby. You focus on Jenny."

"Thanks for sticking around to back me up."

"Happy to help."

Victoria left the office to stash her leftovers in the fridge. She went into the bathroom to wash up and brushed her teeth so she wouldn't knock poor Jenny out with her garlic breath. Then she put her hair back up and stared at her reflection in the mirror. "Where's the magic mirror when you need it?" she asked the familiar face looking back at her.

Even after airing it out with David, she was no closer to a plan than she'd been before. Although she did like his idea to infer that she knew about Fiona without specifically saying so. That would be better than directly confronting Shannon's painful loss. With nothing she could do about her own life at the moment, she went to see to Jenny and the new life she and Alex would welcome into the world tonight.

***

Blaine couldn't stop staring at his baby daughter as she slept in his arms. Everything about her fascinated him, from the quiver of her feathery eyebrows to the purse of her little bow lips to the squeeze of her tiny hand around his finger, he was completely besotted with her.

Adeline... His grandmother would be so pleased when she heard the baby's name. He had a daughter named *Adeline.* Tiffany said they'd call her Addie since Adeline was too much name for a little girl. That was fine with him. After what Tiffany had given him today—and every day since he'd had the good sense to marry her—she could have whatever she wanted.

Tiffany awoke with a groan that had him immediately on alert.

"What's wrong, babe?"

"Everything hurts." She shifted to a different position and winced. "Even my hair hurts. I'd forgotten how bad the aftermath was the first time around."

Still holding the baby, Blaine stood, moving carefully because God forbid he should drop his precious bundle. "Let me see if they can get you something for the pain."

"In a minute. I want to see her first."

He turned so she could see the baby's little face. "Isn't she pretty?"

"She sure is."

"Just like her mama and her sister," he said, leaning over the bed rail to kiss Tiffany. "I'll check with Vic and David about giving you something to make you more comfortable." Reluctantly, he handed the baby over to her, hoping she'd give her back when he returned. He was nowhere near finished holding her.

Blaine went to the desk in the hallway where David and Katie were working on computers.

"How's Tiffany feeling?" Katie asked.

"She's hurting. Is there anything you can give her for that?"

"Absolutely. I'll be in with something in a minute."

"Thank you."

Blaine was heading back to Tiffany's room when a shout from the other end of the long corridor got his attention. Ashleigh broke loose from her aunt Maddie and ran for him. He bent to scoop her up and loved the way she wrapped her arms around his neck and hugged him so hard, he nearly choked.

Laughing, he kissed his stepdaughter's cheek. "Is someone excited to meet her baby sister?"

"What do you think?" Maddie asked when she caught up to them.

"Can I see her?" Ashleigh asked, her green eyes big with excitement. She had her mother's shiny dark hair and exquisite face.

"You certainly can, but you have to be gentle with her and with Mommy, okay? She's tired after having the baby."

"Okay."

Blaine carried her into the room. "We have a very special visitor, Mommy."

"Hey, sweetheart," Tiffany said, lighting up at the sight of her firstborn.

Blaine settled Ash on the bed next to Tiffany and stood back to watch while Ashleigh met her baby sister.

Tiffany gently placed the baby in Ashleigh's arms. "This is Adeline, but we'll call her Addie."

"She's so little!"

"I know, and we have to be extra careful with her."

"I will. I'll take such good care of her."

Blinking back tears, Tiffany looked at Blaine, extending her hand to him.

He went to join his family, taking the hand of the woman who'd given him everything, his heart overflowing with love for all three of his girls.

"Let me get the first picture of the new family," Maddie said, holding her phone. "Get closer to Tiffany, Blaine."

"Nothing I'd rather do," he said with a grin for his wife.

"Put it on ice, buster. No extracurricular activities for six weeks."

"What does that word mean, Mommy?" Ashleigh asked. "Extracrricula."

Blaine cracked up laughing. "Yes, Mommy, what does that mean?"

"It means," Tiffany said with a pointed look for him, "that Blaine has to keep his hands to himself—literally—for six weeks."

He snorted out a laugh at her double meaning.

"They tell us that at camp," Ashleigh said. "You should know that, Blaine, cuz you're a policeman."

"I know, honey," he said with a long-suffering sigh and playful scowl for Tiff. "Don't worry."

"Everybody smile," Maddie said, framing the first picture of the four of them together.

Blaine, who hadn't stopped smiling all day, happily complied and then forwarded the picture Maddie sent him to his family, letting them know Tiffany and the baby would be home tomorrow if they wanted to visit. He had no doubt they'd have a line out the door. His parents had been so excited to see him become a father.

After an hour-long visit that got more exciting when Tiffany's mom and stepfather, Francine and Ned, showed up, Maddie took Ashleigh home with her for a sleepover with her cousins, Thomas and Hailey.

"She's some kind of excited, huh?" Blaine asked Tiffany after everyone had left.

"She's going to be the best big sister ever. Well, except for Maddie, of course."

"Of course. I'm glad Ashleigh has a sister. I know how much you love yours."

"I do love my sister. But you know what this means?"

"What's that?"

"We have to try again to get you a son."

"I don't care about having a son. I love my three girls."

"Still… I may have one more baby in me if you're game."

"You say that now that Katie gave you pain meds. When they wear off, you might not be so agreeable. And PS, I'm always game for making babies with you."

"I want to try for a boy."

"Not today," he said with a teasing grin.

She groaned. "Not any time soon."

"No extracurriculars, Mommy."

"Oh my God! I can't believe she asked me what that meant!"

"I can. She's a parrot. If you say it, she says it."

"I know. It's awful. I have to watch my mouth so closely these days. What if she goes to camp and tells them Mommy and Blaine were talking about extracrricula activities?"

"I'm the police chief, babe. They won't arrest you."

"Thank goodness for that."

Addie came to life with a little squeak that was among the most adorable sounds Blaine had ever heard. "Was Ashleigh like her as a baby? I hate that I missed that time with her."

"She looked just like Addie does, and she used to wake with an indignant squeak, too. I'd forgotten about that."

Addie's squeak quickly became a howl.

"Is someone hungry?" Tiffany asked her new daughter.

"How do you know that?" Blaine asked, fascinated.

"She's not wet, and she just woke up, so she's not tired. Process of elimination."

He watched, enraptured, as she opened the front of her hospital gown and guided the baby to her breast. "That is, without a doubt, the coolest—and *sexiest*—thing I've ever seen in my entire life."

She smiled at him and moved gingerly to one side of the bed. "Come up here with us."

Careful not to jar her, he got on the bed and wrapped his arms around her, letting her lean back against him as she fed the baby.

"Ahhh, that's better," she said with a contented sigh.

"This has been the greatest day of my entire life, Tiffany. Thank you so much for her—and for everything else. You and Ashleigh and now our little Addie… I love you all so much."

With her head resting against his chest, she smiled up at him. "We love you, too. You think I've given you so much, but you've done the same for me. You waited all that time for me to be free."

He ran his finger over her cheek. "Waiting for you—and our family—was the best and smartest thing I ever did."

CHAPTER 4

By the time Jenny was ready to push at one in the morning, Victoria suspected she regretted her decision to forgo pain meds. Jenny was having trouble focusing on her breathing, despite Alex's steady support and encouragement. Her friend Erin Barton had come in around ten and stood by the other side of Jenny's bed, wiping her face with cool cloths and feeding her ice chips to keep her hydrated.

Victoria prepared the bed and the room for delivery, again proceeding through the checklist. She had long ago memorized the steps involved in delivering a baby and went through each one with ruthless attention to detail. Ensuring the safety and comfort of her moms was her top priority along with delivering a healthy baby.

Although it wouldn't be her preference to deliver an older mom on the island, Victoria was determined to make sure the delivery was smooth, and David and Katie were nearby in case she needed them.

She eyed the monitor, watching for the next contraction. "All right, Jenny. Let's get this baby out. On the next contraction, I need a big push."

Jenny pushed for a long, difficult hour before her son emerged into the world, screaming with outrage at the bright lights, the noise and the general inconvenience of leaving the womb. He was absolutely perfect—and close to nine pounds.

"You have a son," Victoria said to Jenny and Alex, who were overcome with emotion. She wiped away a few tears of her own, knowing the long and difficult path Jenny had traveled from losing her fiancé in the World Trade Center on 9/11 to falling for Alex many years later to now becoming a mother.

Katie quickly cleaned up the baby and wrapped him in a receiving blanket before taking him to meet his elated parents and Aunt Erin, who was the twin sister of Jenny's late fiancé.

"Hello, little man," Jenny said softly to the baby, who stared up at her with big dark eyes. He had a smattering of dark hair and his father's olive-toned skin.

"What's his name?" Victoria asked as she tended to Jenny's post-delivery care.

"George Alexander Martinez the second," Jenny said. "After Alex's dad."

"I love that," Erin said. "He looks like a George."

"My dad would be so thrilled," Alex said, wiping away tears.

George let out a lusty cry.

"I think your little guy might be hungry," Victoria said. "Let's see how he takes to breastfeeding."

Two hours later, Victoria was dead on her feet but had two successful deliveries completed and two breastfeeding moms who were doing great. David had checked both babies again, declaring them healthy and strong.

It had been a great day for the clinic team—or was it two days now?

"Go on home," David said to Victoria and Katie. "I'll stay."

Victoria would've argued with him, but his policy was to remain on the premises any time they admitted a patient. Besides, she was so damned tired, she could barely function let alone argue.

"We'll clear your schedule until noon tomorrow," he said. "Sleep in."

"You're the best boss I ever had."

"I love how she says that, as if she's not the boss around here."

Katie laughed. "Seriously."

"Whatever," Victoria said, yawning. "I'm outta here."

"I want my bed and my man," Katie said as she walked with Victoria to the dark parking lot, which held many more cars than usual due to their patients.

"What you said." Victoria's stomach ached at the thought of having to talk to Shannon about what she'd learned about him. But that wasn't going to happen tonight. She'd wait and choose her timing carefully. "Sleep well, and thanks for staying."

"Of course, no problem."

The three of them made a good team, supporting each other through the various challenges they confronted on a daily basis as the island's only medical providers. That they were also great friends made their work environment much more fun and dynamic than it would've been otherwise.

After finishing the Certified Nurse Midwife postgraduate program five years ago, Victoria came to Gansett intending to spend a year gaining experience in midwifery before moving on to something bigger and better. But Gansett had worked its magic on her, and now it felt like home. She thrived on the challenge of providing top-level prenatal care to isolated island moms and liked feeling needed in her professional life.

Now she couldn't imagine living anywhere but on the remote island where she'd found such a satisfying life. That life had become a heck of a lot more satisfying a year ago when Shannon O'Grady arrived.

She drove home to the small house they shared near the Salt Pond, close enough to smell the sea air, which, along with the scenic water views, had become one of her favorite aspects of island life.

Shannon had left the outside light on for her, and she tiptoed inside, hoping she wouldn't wake him. He had an early morning on the ferry.

In the bathroom, she changed into an oversized T-shirt and brushed her teeth before creeping into the bedroom, where she plugged her phone into a bedside charger. She made sure she was always reachable by the expectant moms who depended on her.

When she crawled into bed, Shannon reached for her, the way he did every night when they went to bed together.

"Did I wake you?" she asked.

"Nah, I was dozing, waiting for you."

If she lived forever, she'd never get tired of listening to that lovely accent. She took a deep breath and let it out, aching all over again as she recalled the things Seamus had told her. Thinking about what Shannon had been through broke her heart.

"Long day, love?"

"Long but good with two healthy new babies. Tiffany Taylor had a girl named Adeline, and Jenny Martinez had baby George."

"That's great news."

"It's always a huge relief when island deliveries go well."

"They usually go well when you're involved."

"That's the goal." Yawning, she turned to face him. "How was your day?"

"Less eventful than yours."

Victoria kissed him. "I missed you today."

"Missed you, too. It's not the same around here when you're not home. It's far too quiet. I went over to Seamus's for a little while. It's definitely *not* quiet over there."

She wanted to ask about Jackson and his troubles at camp, but then she'd have to tell him she'd been to see Seamus. So she didn't ask. "That's actually good news. I love to hear the boys are acting like little boys again."

"They certainly are. We played football in the yard with them, and I've got a few new bruises."

"Aww, poor baby."

He slid his leg between hers and tugged her in closer to him. "You could make me feel better."

Victoria laughed at his shameless ploy. Suddenly, she wasn't quite as tired as she'd been a few minutes ago. Being close to him this way always had the same effect on her. If he was nearby, she wanted him. It was one of the simple facts of her life.

"But if you're too tired—"

She kissed him, pouring all the love she felt for him into that single kiss, wishing she could take away the pain he carried with him, even if he never spoke of it.

He rolled her under him, kissing her face and neck.

Victoria wondered if he remembered his lost love when he was with her this way. Did he close his eyes and imagine she was someone else? The thought of that possibility broke her heart and had tears pooling in her eyes that she hoped he wouldn't notice.

They'd come such a long way from the first night they met, or so she'd thought. As he helped her out of the T-shirt she'd worn to bed and left a trail of kisses down the front of her, she thought about the steps they'd taken in the beginning that had led her to believe they were starting a lasting relationship. They'd been tested so they could have sex without condoms and then officially moved in together after spending every night together that first month. Now they shared meals and bills and a bed and a life that had come to mean more to her than anything ever had before.

She'd never lived with a man or engaged in the kind of relationship she had with Shannon. But now she had reason to wonder if they'd been building a life or a house of cards that would collapse under the weight of his past. And why hadn't he told her about Fiona himself? In all the time they'd spent together, how could he have kept such a big part of himself from her?

"Where have you gone off to, love?" he asked, his cock hard against her center.

"I'm here," she said, reaching for him. "I'm right here."

He thrust into her, filling her so completely in every possible way. Her heart overflowed with love for him, with the desire to have everything with him. She wanted little Irish babies who looked just like him and yearned to watch them grow up with him by her side.

Victoria hadn't often entertained those thoughts, because she'd always suspected something was holding him back from fully committing to her. Now that she knew why, it was like the floodgates had opened and all the things she wanted so desperately surged to the surface, making her cling to him as he made love to her.

They'd been together long enough that he sensed something was wrong. "What is it, Vic? Why're you so tense?"

"I'm sorry," she said, unable to let go and relax after the emotionally charged day she'd had. Soon she would have no choice but to do something with the information Seamus had given her. But not now. Not tonight. She wrapped her legs around his waist and ran her fingers through the thick hair that curled at the ends.

"You're sure you're okay?"

"I'm fine. Don't stop."

He grasped her hips and picked up the pace.

Normally, she couldn't form a coherent thought when he was inside her, but tonight, pleasure was no match for the insecurities that filled her mind.

"Tell me you're close, love," he said, sounding tense.

"So close." She wasn't. She'd never faked it before with him. She hadn't had to.

"You feel so good."

Victoria held him tight, fighting the emotional firestorm that threatened to erupt at any second.

"Vic," he said, sounding desperate as he came with a gasp, surging into her.

She couldn't find the wherewithal to pretend she'd come, too. Instead, she caressed his back and continued to run her fingers through his silky hair.

"What's wrong?" he asked after a long silence. "If you were too tired, you could've said so."

"I know. I'm sorry."

"You're not going to tell me what's on your mind?"

"Not now, if that's okay."

He withdrew from her and moved to his back, bringing her with him and arranging her head on his chest, usually her favorite place to sleep. But now she had reason to wonder if the heart that beat so hard and fast belonged to her or if it would forever belong to the woman he'd loved and lost so tragically.

"Whatever it is," he said softly in the voice that touched her soul, "I hope you know you can talk to me."

"I know." Victoria closed her eyes tight against a new flood of tears that wanted out. She felt so raw and exposed, as if her heart were outside her body, unprotected. If she gave in to the tears, she feared they might never stop.

Exhaustion was her savior, dragging her into the oblivion only sleep could provide.

**

It was still dark when Victoria woke to her ringing cell phone. Groaning, she left the warmth of Shannon's embrace to grab the phone, taking it with her to the bathroom, where she closed the door so she wouldn't disturb him.

"This is Victoria."

"It's Luke Harris. I think Syd is in labor. It's come on fast and furious."

"Can you get her to the clinic?"

"I don't think so. She says she needs to push right now."

In the background, Victoria could hear Sydney's anguished cries. "I'll be there in ten minutes."

"Thank you so much."

Victoria ended the call and found David's number on her list of contacts.

"Dr. Lawrence," he muttered.

"David, wake up. Sydney Harris is in labor at home, and it's happening fast. Can you meet me at their place?" She pictured him sacked out on the sofa in his office.

"Yeah."

"Are you awake?"

"I am now."

"Hurry."

"On my way."

Victoria got dressed as fast as she could, took a second to brush her hair and teeth, and then grabbed the bag she kept at home, just in case. It contained some of what they'd need, but not everything. She left a note for Shannon and headed out. From the car, she called Katie.

"Sorry to wake you up, but Sydney Harris is in labor at home. I need a few things from the clinic. Can you help me out?"

"Of course," Katie said, sounding wide awake when she'd been fast asleep one minute ago.

Victoria gave her a list of the supplies she needed.

"Did you call David?"

"He's on his way. I didn't want to slow him down by asking for supplies."

"Understood. I'll be quick."

"Thanks, Katie."

Victoria yawned and glanced at the clock. Quarter to six. She'd gotten about two hours of sleep. Nowhere near enough. Three babies arriving in twenty-four hours was an island record. Fortunately, none of her other expecting moms was close to term, so she should get a break after the Harrises' baby arrived.

She felt a twinge of anxiety about how Sydney's much-anticipated child would enter the world at home and not in the clinic. Like Tiffany and Jenny, Syd had been due to deliver on the mainland in two weeks. But the baby apparently had other plans. Nothing could go wrong with this delivery. There was, Victoria thought, no room for error.

Sydney had lost her first husband and two children in a drunk-driving accident a few years ago. After she married her first love, Luke Harris, Sydney had undergone a procedure to reverse her tubal ligation and had soon conceived what she called her miracle baby. If anyone deserved a miracle, Sydney did, and Victoria was determined to make sure she got one.

Victoria pulled into the Harrises' driveway and parked next to Syd's Volvo. She'd been here a few times for one of the frequent girls' nights out that the island women were so fond of, especially since the guys always crashed. Grabbing her bag, she ran for the door, where Luke greeted her, looking tense and worried.

"Is it bad that the baby is coming so fast?"

"It's not uncommon when it's the mom's third child. Try not to worry."

"That's like telling me not to breathe."

Sydney let out a cry from a bedroom in the back of the house.

"Vic…"

"I know, Luke. We're going to do everything we can for her. David and Katie are on their way. We've got this, but she needs you, too. Get yourself together and come help her."

He nodded and gestured for her to head down the hallway to the bedroom on the left.

After being told that Sydney's first two children had arrived quickly, she'd tried to prepare Sydney—and Luke—for the possibility of that happening again.

"Vic," Syd said, sounding frantic, "the baby is coming."

She was propped up on pillows, towels under her, legs splayed.

On first glance, Victoria could see that the baby was crowning. "When you say fast, you mean it."

"I had a backache all day yesterday. Do you think that was labor?"

"I would say so. Let me wash up, and we'll get that baby out to meet her mom and dad."

"Please hurry. I can't stop it."

Victoria went into the adjoining bathroom to thoroughly wash her hands. Then she donned gloves and a gown before positioning herself between Syd's legs.

Luke came into the room, seeming noticeably calmer than he'd been when he greeted her. "Where do you want me?"

"Behind Syd so you can support her when she pushes."

He got on the bed and took his place behind his wife, gathering her long red hair and smoothing it back from her face.

"On the next contraction, I want you to push," Victoria said. "As hard as you can."

Sydney nodded, and though she looked determined, Victoria could also see a hint of panic.

"Everything's going to be fine, Sydney," Victoria said, praying that was true. "Focus on breathing. Deep breath in. Hold it. Now let it out." She walked her through several more deep breaths before Sydney tensed with the start of the next contraction. "Okay, let's do it."

She'd pushed twice by the time David and Katie arrived.

"We're almost there," Victoria told them. "One more big push, Syd."

With Luke's arms around her, Sydney screamed as she pushed her daughter into the world.

Victoria held her up for her parents to see.

"Oh, Syd," Luke said. "Look at her!"

The baby let out an indignant cry, her face turning red with the rage of being disturbed.

Victoria quickly cut the cord and turned the baby over to David so she could focus on Syd.

"Is she okay?" Luke asked.

"She's perfect," David said. "What's her name?"

"Lillian Alice Harris," Sydney said as tears ran down her face, "after Luke's mom and mine. We're going to call her Lily."

"What a beautiful name," Victoria said.

"My parents are going to be so bummed that they missed this," Syd said. "They're in Wisconsin until next week. So much for their plan to be back for my due date."

"They'll be thrilled to hear she's safely arrived and it all went well," Luke said.

"Yes, they will."

David brought the baby to her elated parents and put her in Sydney's arms.

These were the moments that made Victoria's professional life so very rewarding. She found herself wiping away tears right along with Sydney and Luke, which wasn't uncommon. After spending nearly a year tending to her moms—and their nervous partners—it was always an emotional moment to welcome a new baby, especially one like Lily, who truly was a miracle.

"She's so beautiful, Syd," Luke said. "Just like her mother."

"She looks like you," Syd said.

"No way. God wouldn't be that mean to her."

Everyone laughed.

"She should be so lucky to look like her gorgeous daddy," Syd said, gazing at the baby with amazement and joy that had been a very long time coming.

"Does Syd need to go to the clinic?" Luke asked.

"If you don't mind if I stick around for a couple of hours to keep an eye on both your ladies, they should be able to stay here," Victoria said.

"That's totally fine with us," Luke said.

"I need to get back to the clinic," David said. "We're having a regular baby boom around here."

"We heard Tiffany and Jenny had their babies, too," Luke said.

"I see a big first birthday party in our future a year from now," Katie said.

"I can't believe she's finally here," Sydney said, staring at her daughter.

Luke kept his arms around Syd as she relaxed against him.

Victoria left the room to give them a few minutes alone.

Katie had already left, but David lingered.

"Did you get a chance to talk to Shannon?"

Victoria shook her head. "It was so late when I got home. I didn't want to get into it then. Hopefully, we'll have time to talk later."

"We should be out of the baby delivery business for a while now."

"Let's hope so. Three in twenty-four hours is a new record."

"One I hope we don't beat any time soon." He squeezed her arm. "Call me if you need me—for anything."

"I will. You guys will take care of my appointments today?"

"We've got you covered."

Her absence would make for a busy day for David and Katie, but they could handle the extra appointments.

"Did Tiffany and Jenny have a good night?"

"The babies were up and down, but overall, everyone got some sleep. I'm going to send them all home today."

"Sounds good. Tell them I'll see them in six weeks or sooner if need be."

"Will do." He paused on his way out the door. "So this isn't the time or the place, but Daisy will kill me if I don't get this taken care of."

"Get what taken care of?" Victoria asked, looking up at him in confusion.

"I was supposed to ask you two weeks ago if you'd be in our wedding."

"For real?"

"Yes, for real," he said with exasperation and laughter. "You're one of my best friends and—"

Victoria hurled herself at him, taking him by surprise.

Luckily, he recovered and caught her before they landed on the floor. "Is that a yes?" he asked, laughing.

"Yes! I'd love to be in your wedding. You're one of my best friends, too. Am I a groomsman or a bridesmaid?"

"Bridesmaid," he said. "You'd look silly in a tux."

"No, I wouldn't. I could totally rock a tux."

"I'll let you work that out with Daisy," he said, cuffing her chin on the way out the door.

"David?"

"Yeah?"

"Thanks for asking me. Means a lot."

"Thanks for saying yes."

Victoria smiled and waved as he headed for the driveway. She was so happy for him and Daisy. After the guilt and recriminations he'd suffered through after his engagement to Janey had ended in dramatic fashion after she caught him in bed with another woman, David had worked hard to turn his life around. He'd been so happy since he'd fallen in love with Daisy, and Victoria couldn't wait to dance at their wedding.

While she was truly happy for her friends, she couldn't help but wonder if she'd ever get to dance at her own wedding.

CHAPTER 5

As the first boat off the island cleared the South Harbor breakwater and headed for the mainland, Shannon made his way to the bow, his favorite place to stand during the hour-long ride. He stood at the rail, letting the spray from below wash over him every time the big ferry crested a wave. With his cousin at the helm, Shannon relaxed and took in the scenery as they traveled along the island's rugged north coastline.

He loved this job and the island and the life he'd found there with Victoria, Seamus, Carolina and their vast circle of friends. After a year, Gansett felt like home in a way that Ireland hadn't for quite some time. When he'd accompanied his aunt Nora on her trip to visit Seamus, he certainly hadn't expected to stay when she left to go home.

But he also hadn't expected to meet Victoria his first night on the island. Two weeks later, he'd been nowhere near ready to leave her. He still wasn't, which counted as the biggest surprise of the last year.

Nine years after losing his beloved girlfriend in an act of senseless violence, he was a shell of the man he'd once been. But lately, since he met Vic, to be precise, things had been better. The dark moods didn't come on as often as they used to, and he had new reason to get up in the morning, to function, to put one foot in front of the other and carry on. She'd been perfect for him, a wonderful, sexy companion who didn't ask more of him than he was capable of giving. She would never know how much he appreciated that.

She was off delivering yet another baby. He hadn't heard the phone or her early morning departure. He greatly admired her professional competence and her devotion to her patients. The island's female population was lucky to have her, and they knew it. She was forever coming home with flowers or other gifts her grateful patients had given her.

"Gonna be another scorcher." Shannon immediately recognized the sound of home in his cousin's voice.

"What're you doing up here? You're supposed to be at the helm."

"One of the new captains was hitching a ride back and offered to relieve me. He needs the experience, so here I am."

"Does he know what he's doing?" Shannon asked, eyeing the bridge warily.

Seamus barked out a laugh. "I only hire the best. Not to worry."

"If you say so." His cousin was nothing if not meticulous when it came to running the company owned by Carolina and her son, Joe.

"Vic came to see me yesterday."

Shocked to hear that, Shannon stared at his cousin, almost afraid to ask. "How come?"

"She had some questions."

"About me?"

Seamus nodded.

Shannon's chest felt like it was being compressed by something heavy and unforgiving, the way it had in the days that followed Fiona's death. "What did you tell her?"

"What she needed to know."

"Seamus! *Are you fucking kidding me right now?*"

"Relax. I only gave her the big picture. None of the details."

His mind raced as he tried to absorb the implications. So that was why she'd been so tense last night. "You had no right."

"I had every right. She cares about you. She wants to understand you."

"It's not your place to fill in the blanks for her."

"Whose place is it, then? You're never going to do it."

"How do you know that?"

"It's been a year, Shannon, and she'd never heard Fiona's name."

White-hot rage ripped through him. "And now she has?"

"Now she has."

"It wasn't your place! I can't believe you'd interfere in my life this way! What gives you the right?"

"The woman who loves you asked me. That's what gave me the right."

"She doesn't love me. She enjoys fucking me. Big difference."

"You're a bloody fool if that's what you think. Open your goddamned eyes and look at what's right in front of you before she gets tired of competing with a ghost she didn't even know about and walks away."

Shannon didn't think before he reacted, punching his cousin in the face so hard that pain radiated from his hand up his arm.

Seamus went flying backward, falling hard against one of the benches and landing on the deck. For the longest time, he didn't move, and for a brief, terrifying second, Shannon feared he'd killed his cousin.

Filled with unreasonable terror, Shannon leaned over him. "Seamus, I'm sorry!" He shook his shoulder. "Seamus! Wake up!" They'd attracted a crowd of curious onlookers, including several of Shannon's fellow deckhands. "Please wake up."

"Quit yer bellowing," Seamus said without opening his eyes. The left side of his face was already swelling and turning purple.

"I'm sorry. I shouldn't have... I don't know why..."

Seamus held up his hand, opening the eye that still worked. "Stop talking and help me up."

Shannon took hold of his cousin's hand and hauled him to his feet, grasping his shoulder when Seamus wavered.

"Show's over, folks," Seamus said. "Move along."

"Go get some ice," Shannon said to one of the guys he worked with. "Hurry." He helped Seamus onto the bench. "I'm really sorry."

"I heard you the first time."

His colleague Mark returned with a bag of ice that he handed to Seamus, who applied it to his face. "Sit yer arse down," Seamus said to Shannon when they were alone again.

Shannon sat next to him on the bench.

"You've put me in an awkward situation here. Because half the crew saw you hit me, I have no choice but to suspend you for three days for disciplinary reasons. An official note will be placed in your employee file. In this company, it's two strikes and you're out—cousin or not."

Knowing he'd fucked up, Shannon took a deep breath and let it out. "Okay."

"I want to say something else, and I want you to *listen* to me." Seamus removed the ice from his bruised face. "For nine long years, we've stood by you and tried to support you as best we could through an unimaginable tragedy. In the last year, I've seen you come back to life, back to the man you were before you lost Fi. That's *because* of Victoria. You lost Fiona through no fault of your own. If you push Victoria away because she's gotten too close, that'll be your own tough shit."

Taking the ice bag with him, Seamus got up and walked away.

Filled with despair the likes of which he hadn't felt so deeply in years, Shannon watched him go.

***

"I'm seriously in awe of you," Luke said to Syd late that afternoon, after Victoria had declared both ladies to be in perfect health and left them alone to care for their new baby. Lily—he had a *daughter* named *Lily*—was asleep in her bassinette next to their bed.

"Is that right?" Syd said with a saucy smile. Before Victoria left, he'd helped Sydney take a shower and gotten her settled back in bed while Victoria watched the baby.

Though Sydney was exhausted, her eyes were alight with joy. "Mmm," he said, nuzzling her neck. "That's right. You amaze me. After months of planning and me stressing out about all the things that could go wrong, you go and give birth without even leaving our bed."

Sydney laughed. "Well, that wasn't exactly the plan."

"I'm still allowed to be amazed."

"I'm just glad she's here safely, and we didn't have to leave the island to have her."

"Do you think she'll always be so accommodating of her parents?"

"Doubtful. I expect her to be a strong-willed girl like her sister was."

"That'd be fine with me, as long as you promise to protect me during the teenage years, when my little princess turns into a demon child."

She patted his head. "I'll run interference. Don't worry."

"Sometimes I still can't believe…" His throat tightened and his eyes filled. He'd been an emotional disaster all day.

"What can't you believe?"

"That you came back. That you actually love me and agreed to marry me and have given me a daughter. I was so alone for such a long time… And now…" He caressed her face and gently kissed her. "Now, I have everything."

"I don't even like to think about what I'd be doing if I hadn't come to the island or if you hadn't come to find me."

"Don't you mean if I hadn't spied on you?" he asked with a chuckle.

"It doesn't count as spying if I knew you were there. The scrape of your boat landing on the beach was one of the most familiar sounds in my life back when we were first together. I used to listen for it every night."

"Best thing I ever did was row my boat to your beach, baby," he said with a lascivious grin.

Sydney laughed at the double meaning behind his words. "You're going to make sure I'm not a total freak show with her, right?"

"Of course I am."

"I don't want her to grow up to be afraid of everything the way I am now."

"You're not giving yourself enough credit, honey. Look at what you've already done to prove you're not afraid of what might happen."

"What do you mean?"

"You married me. You had the tubal ligation reversed. You allowed me to knock you up, which was a great pleasure, I might add. You've given birth to a new baby. To me, all those things indicate your tremendous courage, not debilitating fear."

"That's nice of you to say, but the fear is still there. Maybe I just hide it better than I used to."

"I'm not just spewing platitudes here, Syd. I mean it when I say you're not giving yourself enough credit. You aren't the same fearful person you were when we first got back together. You've come a long way from there. Maybe you can't see it, but I do."

"If that's true, it's because of you. Your love has given me the strength to go on, to be optimistic and hopeful and joyful and all the things I thought I'd never be again after I lost Seth and the kids."

Luke leaned in to kiss her. "Whatever I've given you is a fraction of what I've gotten back in return."

Her smile lit up her gorgeous blue eyes. "I was thinking…"

"About?"

"This one went pretty well. Easy conception, uneventful pregnancy and delivery…"

His heart stopped beating for a second. "What're you saying?"

"Maybe we ought to do it one more time so Lily doesn't grow up alone."

Luke stared at her, incredulous. They'd agreed that one child would be a miracle. The thought of another was almost more than he could process.

Sydney waved her hand in front of his face. "Earth to Luke. Have I totally shocked you?"

"No, sweetheart, you've totally thrilled me."

"So you'd be game for doing this again?"

"Anything you want. Anything at all."

"Hmm," she said, her expression mischievous, "that's a pretty big mandate you're giving me."

"It's a pretty big love I have for you."

Moving slowly and carefully, Sydney snuggled up to him, and Luke wrapped his arms around her, profoundly relieved to have the delivery behind them and a lifetime to look forward to with Sydney and Lily and whoever might come next.

***

After leaving the Harrises', Victoria spent a few hours at the clinic, helping David prepare Tiffany and Jenny to take their babies home. Jenny was having some challenges with breastfeeding, so Victoria spent an hour trying to help. She was so tired that her brain was actually buzzing from the lack of sleep.

"Go home," David said at two. "Before you fall over and become a patient."

"I'm going." Victoria didn't have the energy to argue with him. "Back to business as usual tomorrow."

"Let's hope so."

Victoria drove home with the windows open, hoping the fresh air would keep her awake long enough to make it safely to her driveway. She couldn't recall the last time she'd been this tired. Well, maybe the week she met Shannon when they'd stayed up every night for days because they'd been having too much fun to sleep.

Thinking about those first days together made her smile. That had been the most exciting time, to have found someone who captivated her so completely. That was all she'd ever wanted for her personal life, a man who loved her as much as she loved him and to live happily ever after with him. Was that too much to ask?

This time yesterday, she would've said she and Shannon had laid the foundation for that kind of relationship. Now she wasn't sure of anything.

When she pulled into the driveway, she was surprised to see his motorcycle parked outside. He was supposed to be at work. What the hell? She got out of the car and went inside, where he was seated at the kitchen table, an ice pack on his hand.

"Hey," she said. "What's wrong?"

He looked up at her, his eyes bleak. "Got into a fight at work. They sent me home for three days."

Stunned, she said, "A fight about what?"

"If it's okay, I'd rather not talk about it."

"Oh," she said, stung by his dismissive tone. "Okay. I'm… ah… just going to get some sleep, then."

He nodded and returned his attention to his injured hand.

Victoria went into the bathroom and numbly went through the motions of changing into a T-shirt and brushing her teeth. In the bedroom, she closed the blinds and got into bed, staring up at the ceiling while trying to make sense of what he'd told her.

He'd gotten into a fight. Her Shannon, a pacifist down to his bones, had actually gotten into a *fight* at work and was sent home for *three days*. What the heck could've precipitated that? And why wouldn't he tell her what happened?

She, who had been thoroughly exhausted ten minutes ago, was now so wired she couldn't sleep. How was it possible that in just twenty-four hours, her entire world had been turned upside down? Why hadn't she left well enough alone and resisted the temptation to ask questions of Seamus? Now she had information she didn't know what to do with, and Shannon was getting into fights. Coincidence? Probably not.

Oh God. What if he'd fought with Seamus? The possibility had her sitting up in bed, reeling from the potential implications of Shannon fighting with a man who was not only his boss but also his cousin. Was that what'd happened?

Victoria got out of bed and went to the kitchen to find the chair he'd recently occupied now empty.

Outside, the roar of his bike starting up had her running for the door, but she was too late. He was gone by the time she made it outside. Where was he going, and when would he be back?

Victoria went inside, but she was far too agitated to sleep. She needed answers, and she needed them now. Instead of going back to bed, she got dressed and shoved her feet into flip-flops, grabbing her purse and keys on the way out the door.

Mindful of her lack of sleep, Victoria made an effort to concentrate on her driving and not on the turmoil roiling inside her. She took a right turn into a driveway that had become familiar to her in the last year after many visits and parked next to Seamus's truck. In the yard, Kyle and Jackson were playing with their dog, laughing and running around the way little boys ought to.

Victoria waved to them on her way to the house, where she knocked on the back door.

Carolina came to the door and didn't seem surprised to see her. "Come in."

Her stomach aching with nerves, Victoria followed her into the kitchen, stopping short at the sight of Seamus's badly bruised and swollen face. For a long moment, she couldn't bring herself to move. She could only stare.

"Come in, Vic," Seamus said. "Looks worse than it is."

"It's all my fault," she said, her voice rough with emotion. "I never should've come to you. If I hadn't… He never would've… This…"

Seamus got up and came over to her. "It's *not* your fault."

"You two fought because you told me about Fiona. That's why, right?"

"We fought because he didn't like something I said to him."

"But it started because I went to you with questions I should've asked him." Blinded by tears, Victoria wiped her cheek with the back of her hand.

Carolina came to her, put her hands on Victoria's shoulders and guided her to a seat at the table. "You didn't throw the punch," she said.

"I started the fight, though," Victoria said.

"No, you didn't," Seamus said. "I pushed him too far."

Carolina raised the ice bag to his face and held it in place. "That doesn't give him the right to punch you."

"I've made such a mess of things," Victoria said. "I should've left well enough alone."

"If you'd done that, your relationship with him never would've been more than what it is right now," Seamus said. "I was under the impression you wanted it to be more."

"I did. I *do*. But not if it's going to cause this kind of trouble."

"You were trying to understand him better by going to Seamus," Carolina said. "You had no way to know the magnitude of what you were going to be told or how he'd react to hearing that Seamus told you. Your intentions were pure and came from a place of love. No one can fault you for that."

Carolina's softly spoken words broke something in Victoria, the core of strength that had been holding her together since learning of Shannon's tragic past. She dropped her head into her hands as her body shook with sobs, her heart broken for Shannon's loss as much as her worries about her own future with him.

A few minutes later, the unmistakable roar of Shannon's motorcycle outside had Victoria hurrying to dry her face and wipe her eyes with the tissue Carolina handed her.

Seamus put the ice bag on the table. "Let me handle this." He stalked to the door and went outside.

CHAPTER 6

The slam of the screen door closing startled Victoria out of the daze she'd fallen into. She got up to follow Seamus, who had Shannon by the arm in the yard.

"Wait," she cried. "*Stop*. Just stop!" She forced her way between the cousins and took hold of Shannon's arm. "Walk away. Right now." She marched him toward the path that led from the yard to the rugged coastline.

Jackson and Kyle stood off to the side, watching them go by with big eyes.

Victoria felt bad for bringing their drama to Seamus and Carolina's home.

"What're you doing here?" Shannon asked when they had left the yard behind.

"About two seconds after you left, I figured out who you fought with at work, and I came to check on him."

"You're awfully cozy with my cousin all of a sudden."

Victoria gave him a hard shove that he didn't see coming, making him stumble on the dirt path. "Shut up. I am not *cozy* with him. I am *friends* with him *through you*, as you well know."

When he turned to face her, she was taken aback by the stormy expression on his face. In all their time together, she'd never seen that particular look on him before. "I don't know who you think you are, poking your nose into stuff that's none of your business."

"*None of my business?* How do you figure it's none of my business when you're *living in my house and sleeping in my bed*?"

"Both of which can be easily rectified."

Stunned by the hostile rebuke, Victoria reeled from the meaning behind his words. "So that's how you're going to play this? You're going to run away because I wanted to know why we're stuck in the same place we were a year ago?"

"*That's* what you think? That we're in the same place we were a year ago?" He shook his head in disbelief.

"We're exactly where we were then. We haven't taken a single step forward from the day you moved in."

"That is not true," he said softly.

She couldn't miss the hint of sadness in his tone. "Shannon—"

He held up a hand to stop her. "I can't do this."

A shockingly painful bolt of fear jolted her. "What can't you do?"

"This. Any of it. I never should've… I can't." He brushed by her and started back up the path toward the yard.

"Shannon, wait! You can't just walk away from me after everything we've shared."

He whirled around. "According to you, we haven't shared anything."

"I never said that!"

"Didn't you?"

When he started walking again, she chased after him, grabbing his shirt and forcing him to stop.

"I never said that."

"What did you say, then, Vic? Explain it to me."

She swallowed the huge lump in her throat and tried to ignore the roar in her ears and the relentless beat of her heart so she could focus on him. "I said we are stuck in the same place we started. That's all."

"I don't know how you can say that." He raised his hands to his head and ran his fingers roughly through his hair, leaving it standing on end.

She had to resist the urge to straighten it the way she would have only yesterday, before she ruined everything by digging into his past.

"If you think that," he said, "you don't know me at all."

"I *want* to know you. Why do you think I went to Seamus in the first place? It's because I want that so badly."

"So badly that you couldn't ask me what you wanted to know?"

He had her there. "I was afraid to."

Seeming stunned, he stared at her. "You were *afraid* to talk to me? What the hell, Victoria?"

"I don't know why I felt that way. I guess I figured if you were ever going to tell me what was holding you back from fully committing to me, you would've by now."

"Fully committing," he said with a huff of incredulous laughter. "I live with you. I sleep with you. I have sex with you almost every day, sometimes twice a day. How do *you* define fully committed?"

Victoria had to fight the need to squirm under his intense green-eyed gaze. "Is that it? Is that going to be our life? Living together, sleeping together, having sex?"

"I thought you *liked* our life."

"I do!"

"Then what in the name of God is the problem, Victoria?"

"I…" She took a deep breath and forced herself to meet his gaze. "I want more."

Again she saw sadness and weary resignation in his expressive eyes. "I'm not capable of more."

"Yes, you are."

"No, Victoria, I'm really not. I like what we have. It works for me. If it's not working for you, all you have to do is say so."

"It does work for me, but—"

"No buts. It either works for you or it doesn't. Which is it?"

She once again swallowed a lump in her throat as a hundred scenarios flashed through her mind in the span of a second. One thing became crystal clear—if they weren't together, they'd never be able to move forward. Right here, right now, preserving the relationship they already had was her top priority.

"Vic? What's it going to be?"

"It works for me."

"No more poking around in my past, you got me?"

"Were you ever going to tell me about it?"

"No."

"Just no? That's it?"

"Just no. That's it." As he said those words, she saw more passion and fire in his eyes than she had ever seen before—and all of it for a woman who had died.

Something inside *her* died at realizing she couldn't compete with that woman. She couldn't—and wouldn't—compete with her. "I… I'm sorry. It turns out that this isn't going to work for me after all."

"What're you saying?"

Since she might not get another chance, Victoria decided it was time to lay it all on the line. "I love you, Shannon. I'm in love with you. I want a life with you. I want us to have so much more than a shared address, a shared bed and the best sex I've ever had. I want a family. I want kids and a husband and a commitment from a man who loves me and only me. I want the fairy tale."

"I'm not capable of fairy tales."

"Yes, you are!" She closed the distance between them, placing her hands on his chest and sliding them up to encircle his neck. "You're so capable. You're everything I want and need. All you have to do is be willing to accept what I want to give you and then give it back to me."

"I can't," he said, shaking his head. "I can't. I'm sorry. If I was going to have that with anyone, it would be you."

"Shannon, please. All I'm asking you to do is *try*."

"I have tried. I've tried my best for a year, and you're telling me that my best isn't enough for you."

"Talk to me about her. Tell me what happened. Let me share your burden."

He pulled free of her. "I don't talk about her. I hate that you even know about her."

"Why don't you want me to know? What do you think I'll do with that information besides love you more than I already do?"

Shaking his head, he said, "Don't love me, Vic. I'm not worth it."

"It's far, *far* too late to tell me that." After taking a moment to summon the courage she needed, she looked him in the eye and lowered her voice in case little ears were nearby. "I know how to turn you on and just how to touch you to make you shout when you come. I know what makes you tremble and what makes you sigh with pleasure, but I didn't know about the most important person in your life until someone else told me about her. I don't know what you hope for, what you dream about, what you *want* for yourself. All I'm asking for is the chance to know *you*, Shannon, not just what turns you on."

He broke the intense eye contact and looked down at the ground. After a long moment, he finally returned his gaze to her, seeming devastated by what she'd said. "I'm sorry to have disappointed you this way. I never intended for that to happen. Jesus, I never intended for any of this to happen." He caressed her face, his touch electrifying her as it always did. Then he kissed her forehead. "Give me an hour, and I'll be out of the house. I'm so sorry, love."

Riveted by the sight of him walking away from her, Victoria stood there until long after he'd disappeared around a bend in the path. Tears rolled unchecked down her face as she tried to process what'd just happened. He'd ended it with her rather than share himself, his past, his pain or his love with her.

Her chest tightened, the ache centered in her heart, which had been shattered in the scope of a few minutes. Blinded by tears, she bent at the waist, trying to force air into lungs that felt compressed by the magnitude of the pain. Nothing had ever hurt like this did.

Victoria had no idea how long she was there before she heard Seamus say her name.

"Come with me," he said, helping her to stand upright and guiding her toward his home with his arm around her shoulders.

Victoria pressed her face against his chest and let him lead the way for her. She was incapable of even the simplest things at the moment. He settled her on the sofa in their sitting room. Even though it was summer and hot outside, she shivered uncontrollably. Seamus pulled a blanket over her and then sat on the edge of the sofa.

"There now," he said in that hauntingly beautiful accent. "It's going to be okay."

Victoria shook her head. She had a hard time believing anything was ever going to be okay again.

"There's an old saying… I can't remember who said it, but it went something like this. If you love someone, set them free. If they come back to you, they're yours. If they don't, they never were."

A sob hiccupped through her, and tears fell in a steady stream. She already knew that Shannon wouldn't come back. He'd never been hers. She just hadn't understood that before now. "I… I should go. You don't need this here. The boys—"

"Are fine, and you're welcome here for as long as you'd like to stay." He pulled the blanket up farther. "Close your eyes and try to rest for a bit. You're in no condition to drive."

Victoria knew she ought to get up and go home to her own house to mourn in private, but she couldn't seem to make her body heed the call to move. So she stayed put on Seamus and Carolina's sofa and cried herself to sleep.

CHAPTER 7

Shannon guided the motorcycle out of Seamus's driveway and drove much faster than he should have on the island's winding roads, the careless disregard for his own safety an unwelcome reminder of the years that followed Fiona's death when he hadn't given a flying fuck about anything, least of all himself.

A jumble of mixed emotions assailed him—anger, grief, sadness, frustration and love. Yes, he loved Victoria. How could he not? She was amazing, sweet, sexy, smart and funny. They'd had an incredible year together, or so he'd thought. Apparently, it hadn't been as great for her, which was a huge surprise to him. He'd had no idea she was in any way unhappy until Seamus told him she'd been asking about his past.

No, he did *not* want to talk about Fiona. It had taken him years to be able to take a deep breath around the searing, agonizing pain in his chest after she died. It had taken years to be able to do anything other than relentlessly grieve. The last fecking thing in the goddamned world he wanted to do was talk about Fiona or what it'd been like to lose her. That would be like pouring battery acid on a festering wound that had never truly healed—and never truly would.

Crushed shells crunched under his tires as he pulled into the driveway at the home he'd shared with Victoria. It had been a good year, the best one he'd had since losing Fi. He'd never deny that or even try to. Vic said she wanted more. He didn't have more to give. It was that simple.

He parked the bike and went inside, where the familiar scent of home greeted him. Vic fancied her candles and smelly things. The memory of teasing her about a candle that smelled like laundry detergent stopped him in his tracks, the same way a punch to the gut would. Closing his eyes, he took a deep breath and let it out slowly, but that couldn't keep the old familiar despair from creeping up on him. He'd woken up this morning thinking everything was fine and now… Now it was a fecking mess again.

Life with Victoria had been peaceful and sweet and… *Fuck*, he was going to miss her. He sat down hard on the bed they'd shared for so many blissful nights and dropped his head into his hands. This, right here, was why he'd once vowed to never get involved with a woman again. Who needed this kind of pain when it ended? And it always ended.

Running his fingers through his hair, he thought about arriving on Gansett Island, meeting Victoria that first night and being instantly wowed by her. The first thing he'd noticed was her smile and the way it lit up her entire face. Her pervasive joyfulness had soothed him from the beginning. It hadn't taken long for him to become addicted to her joy and the way he felt when he was around her.

He hadn't come to Gansett looking for anything more than a couple of weeks away from the memories and the ghosts that had haunted him for the long years since Fiona was taken from him. To say that his relationship with Victoria had been a huge surprise was putting it mildly. Out of sheer necessity, he'd been with other women since he lost Fi, but Victoria had been the first relationship he'd had, and now that too was gone, leaving yet another gaping wound for him to contend with.

How many such wounds could one heart withstand in a lifetime and still beat the way it was supposed to?

Reaching under the bed, he pulled out the duffel bag he'd stashed there when he moved in and tossed it on the bed. Without thinking too much about what he was doing, he emptied the two drawers Vic had made available to him in her dresser and retrieved his shaving bag from the bathroom. Then he went to the closet to retrieve the few items he had on hangers and came face-to-face with the sexy black dress Victoria had worn to Dan and Kara's wedding earlier in the month. God, she'd looked beautiful that day.

He recalled being eager to get her home the whole time they were at the wedding and thought about slow dancing with her to one song after another. Then he'd watched her crazy antics on the dance floor with the other women to the faster songs. At the time, he'd thought she was life personified—energy, intelligence, beauty and joy. He kept coming back to that word when he thought of Victoria. In recent years, he'd had so little to be joyful about that it had been the first of many things that'd attracted him to her.

"Ah, bollox," he muttered to the empty house. "What does it matter now what attracted you to her? It's over. You've seen to that."

Ten minutes after he began, he was completely packed, which made him realize that for all the time he'd spent in this house, he'd done almost nothing to make it his home as much as it was hers. Probably because he'd known, in his heart of hearts, that he wouldn't be here forever.

In the kitchen, he put down his bag and peeled the key she'd given him when he moved in off his ring, placing it on the table. His entire body ached with regret as he stared down at that key and everything it stood for, remembering the hopeful, excited expression on her face when she'd given it to him after he decided to stay on at the end of his two-week vacation. At the time, he'd figured he'd be here a month, maybe two. Now here it was a year later, and he'd found a whole new life here with a job he enjoyed, new friends and...

Sighing, he picked up his bag. The best part of his new life on Gansett was over now, and he'd have to find a way to accept that and move on. He pulled the door closed behind him and made sure it was locked. As he was strapping the duffel onto the back of his bike, his phone rang. Seeing the call was from Seamus, he took it.

"Hey," he said.

"Did you move out of Vic's?"

"Yeah."

"The company has a room at the Beachcomber. I left word at the desk that it's okay for you to stay there."

"I… um… Why are you helping me out after what I did today?"

"Because you're still my cousin, and I still care about you even if I think you're being an absolute gobshite to walk away from the woman who loves you."

Shannon closed his eyes against the burn of tears that infuriated him. He refused to be sucked into the bottomless rabbit hole of grief once again. "I know it's not possible for you to understand, but this is what's best for me right now."

"Fair enough."

"Seamus… I'm really sorry again about today. You've been… really good to me through all of it, and you deserve better from me than what you got from me today."

"And I'm sorry if I overstepped by talking to Vic, but I like her for you. I've enjoyed seeing you happy again after a long dark winter filled with despair."

Shannon's throat closed around a lump. He closed his eyes tight and tried to contain the rush of emotion. Everything his cousin had said was true, but none of it changed the simple fact that Shannon was no longer capable of the level of intimacy that Victoria needed and deserved from the man in her life. For the first time since he lost Fiona, he wished he could be different or more or whatever Victoria needed to make her happy. But that wasn't possible.

"Call me if you need anything," Seamus said.

His cousin's generosity in light of the day's events only added to the weight pressing on Shannon's chest. "I will. Thanks."

He stashed the phone in his pocket and straddled the bike, taking a long last look at the little house where he'd lived with Victoria. Seamus was right—he had been happy with her. He'd never deny that, but one of the reasons he'd been so happy was that she'd never asked for more than he had to give.

Until now.

Kick-starting the bike, he turned it toward the road and left behind the house he'd called home for the last year, weary at the thought of starting over.

Again.

***

Victoria woke to darkness, low voices and the giggles of little boys trying to be quiet. For a moment, she couldn't recall why she'd been sleeping in Seamus and Carolina's sitting room, but then it all came flooding back in a wave of painful memories that took her breath away.

Shannon was gone. Their relationship was over.

As she remembered their heated exchange in the yard and the despair she'd seen in his eyes, it literally hurt to breathe.

She gave herself a few minutes to get it together before she sat up, ran her fingers through her hair and hoped her ravaged face wouldn't scare the boys. After folding the blanket Seamus had covered her with and putting it over the back of the sofa, she took a deep breath and braced herself to face her friends.

The four of them were seated around the table eating hamburgers and french fries. Jackson had ketchup on his cheek, and Kyle was talking with his mouth full while Carolina gently corrected his manners. They made for such a sweet little family, and Victoria admired Seamus and Caro tremendously for what they'd done for the boys.

"She's awake!" Kyle cried when he saw Victoria. "Can we be loud now?"

Seamus laughed at the question and the mouthful of food that nearly fell from Kyle's face as he spoke. "Close yer mouth and chew."

"I'm so sorry you had to be quiet for me," Victoria said to Kyle.

"Hope you had a good nap," Seamus said, studying her with concern on a face that was almost as handsome as his younger cousin's, even when bruised and swollen. She would always be partial to Shannon's handsome face, whether they were together or not.

"I did. Thank you so much for letting me stay. I'll get out of your hair now."

"You're not in our hair," Carolina said. "How about something to eat?"

Victoria placed a hand on her abdomen. "I don't think I could, but thank you anyway."

Carolina stood to hug her. "Hang in there, and if you need us, you have friends here."

"Thank you," Victoria said softly, afraid to say anything more than that due to her shaky composure.

"I'll walk you out," Seamus said.

Victoria waved to the boys and preceded Seamus out the door. When she reached her car, she turned to him. "Thank you for everything. You went above and beyond. I'm sorry that I put you in this position to start with. I never should've come to you yesterday."

"That's a load of shite. You didn't do anything wrong. You wanted insight. Who else should you have asked if you didn't feel comfortable asking him?"

"That's just it, though. If I didn't feel comfortable asking him, that should've been a sign to me that something was wrong."

"Maybe so, but your heart was in the right place trying to figure him out. And you suspected there were things he was keeping from you that would matter at some point."

Victoria ran her hand over the heart that ached from the loss of the man she loved. "How long will it hurt this bad?"

"For a while, I suspect. After Caro and I first got together, she decided our age difference was too much for her to take on. We went round and round for quite some time until I couldn't take it anymore. I actually gave Joe my notice, intending to go home to Ireland, because I couldn't be here if I couldn't have her."

"I had no idea you guys went through all that."

"Aye, it was a terrible situation for a long time. I know what it's like to have your heart feel like it's cracked down the middle and nothing can fix it except the one you love."

"What happened? How did you end up staying?"

"Joe told his mum that I'd given notice, and that night she came to find me, asking me not to go—and not because my departure would create a nightmare at work for her son, but because she wanted me to stay. What started out as one of the worst days of my life turned into one of the best." He drew Victoria into a hug. "I know it's awful right now, but don't give up hope. This break might be just what he needs to get his head out of his arse and see what's right in front of him."

Though she wanted to cling to Seamus's hopeful thought with everything she had, Victoria also had to be realistic. "I don't think that's going to happen, but I appreciate you trying to cheer me up."

He released her from his embrace. "You heard what Caro said. We're your friends. If you need us, you know where we are."

Victoria kissed the cheek that wasn't bruised. "Thank you." She got into the car and put down the window.

"Incidentally," Seamus said, "Shannon is staying in the ferry company's room at the Beachcomber. Just in case he left anything behind at your place."

"Good to know," she said, swallowing hard at the realization that he was already long gone from their home.

"I'll check on you tomorrow."

"Hey, Seamus? Carolina was smart to go after you."

"I know," he said with a shit-eating grin. "That's another thing I tell her every day."

Smiling, Victoria waved as she drove down the driveway toward the main road that looped around the island. At the point where she had to decide whether to go right to go home, she faced a quandary. The thought of going to her place to confront Shannon's glaring absence made her feel even sicker than she already did, so she took a left and headed for David's.

On the way, she called him to see if he and Daisy were home. He answered on the third ring, sounding out of breath.

"Hey, what's up?" he said.

"I was wondering if you're home, but it sounds like I might be interrupting something."

"Ha, very funny. I ran for the phone because I was over at Jared's and forgot to bring it with me. Daisy heard it ringing. So yes, I'm home."

"Do you mind if I come over and maybe borrow your sofa tonight?" As she asked the question, Victoria felt pathetic for being so needy, but she simply couldn't face her empty house. Not tonight anyway.

"Of course. Our sofa is your sofa."

"I'll be there in a few."

"Sounds good."

Victoria again had to remind herself to concentrate on her driving so she wouldn't end up in a ditch or worse, off the side of one of Gansett's many sheer cliffs. Somehow she managed to navigate the island's winding roads and arrive safely at the driveway to David's home.

Looking like the cute engaged couple they were, David and Daisy both waited for her, sitting on the steps to their apartment over the garage at Jared and Lizzie James's waterfront estate. Victoria cut the engine and tried to find the wherewithal to get out of the car, determined to keep it together until she could be alone again.

Her resolve lasted until David got up and came over to her, wrapping his arms around her.

Victoria broke down into heartbroken sobs.

To his credit, David said nothing. He only held her while she cried it out. Then he kept an arm around her while he walked her inside with Daisy leading the way.

"I'm sorry to barge in on you guys this way," Victoria said, wiping away her tears. "But Shannon moved out, and I didn't want to be there tonight."

"You didn't barge in on us," Daisy said, "and of course you should come to us. I don't blame you for not wanting to be at home tonight. I'm sorry to hear about you and Shannon."

"I guess your talk with him didn't go well," David said.

She filled them in on Shannon's fight with Seamus and the conversation that had led to their breakup.

"Dear God," Daisy said. "His girlfriend was *murdered?*"

Victoria nodded as she sank to the sofa, her legs feeling less than supportive. "Nine years ago."

"You've known all along there was something," David said, sitting next to her on the sofa while Daisy took one of the chairs. "I remember a few times when you've wondered whether he would ever want more with you."

"There was definitely a wall that I kept butting up against," Victoria said, swiping impatiently at tears that refused to quit. "And now that wall has a name, and I'm so heartbroken for her and for him."

Daisy got up and retrieved a box of tissues that she handed to Victoria. Then she sat on the other side of Victoria on the sofa.

Victoria sent her a grateful smile. Thank goodness for friends at a time like this. She wiped her face and blew her nose. "What does it say about me that this is the first time in my life that I have ever cried over a guy?"

"It says to me that you've been very, very lucky," Daisy said.

Victoria immediately felt like total shit for saying such a thing, knowing that Daisy had been beaten by the last man she'd been involved with before David. "I'm sorry, Daisy. That was insensitive."

"No need to apologize. I mean it when I say you're lucky if this is the first time you've cried over a guy. I've been crying over them for most of my adult life."

"Until recently," David said, smiling at her.

"Now they're all happy tears," Daisy said, returning her fiancé's smile.

"I want what you guys have," Victoria said. "Is that too much to wish for?"

"Not at all," Daisy said, hugging her with one arm.

"I never should've gone to Seamus," Victoria said, filled with regret over the thing that had led to their breakup. "If only I hadn't done that."

"If you hadn't," David said, "you never would've known what'd happened to Shannon, because he wasn't about to tell you, and you also never would've had what you really want with him. You've been chafing at the bit with him for a while now, Vic. Much to my dismay, you used to joke, *frequently*, about how you two were all about the hot sex. Lately, you haven't been making those jokes. You've been dissatisfied. We've both noticed that."

Daisy nodded in agreement.

"I thought I did a better job of hiding it from everyone."

"We know you too well," David said. "I saw it happening months ago."

"I kept hoping if maybe I stuck it out long enough, that he'd open up to me," she said softly. "I gave him so many chances, but he never did."

"And he wasn't going to," David said. "You were right to force the issue. It was either that or spend forever in this odd state of limbo."

"Well, I got what I was looking for. Some of it, anyway. Not that it matters now."

"It matters, Vic," Daisy said. "You love him, and I believe he loves you, too. I've seen the way he looks at you. If that's not a man in love, then I know nothing about love."

"And she knows love," David said in all seriousness. "Trust me on that."

Both women laughed.

"It helps to know you think he feels that way about me," Victoria said to Daisy.

"I'm not just saying what you need to hear. I believe it. Give him some time to see what life without you is like. He'll be back."

"I guess we'll see, won't we?"

David put his arm around her. "You're welcome to stay with us for as long as you want."

Victoria leaned her head on his shoulder. "The last thing you lovebirds need is me sitting between you."

"We don't mind," Daisy said.

"I can't stand to see you so sad," David said. "I like it much better when you're busting my balls or telling me inappropriate details about your sex life."

Victoria laughed even as she battled more tears. "You won't need to worry about inappropriate details for a while."

"I know it doesn't seem like it now, but you're going to get through this," David said. "I promise."

"Keep telling me that."

"Any time you need to hear it."

"How about something to eat?" Daisy asked.

"I'm not sure I could."

"Cereal?" David asked. "You never say no to that."

Victoria was about to decline when her stomach growled—loudly.

Laughing, David said, "I'll take that as a yes. Come on." He took her hand and pulled her up, towing her along to the kitchen. "Daisy got me Cap'n Crunch."

Suddenly, there was nothing she'd rather do than eat Cap'n Crunch with David. "She really does love you."

"She certainly does."

***

While Daisy got Victoria settled on the sofa, David took a shower and thought about the terrible situation his friend had found herself in. He had no doubt whatsoever that Vic loved Shannon and had for quite some time. That said, however, he'd been increasingly concerned by Shannon's seeming inability to commit to anything more than what appeared, from the outside looking in, to be a somewhat casual domestic arrangement. Knowing Victoria wanted and needed more than that, David had worried about her getting hurt.

It was, he'd discovered, a tricky proposition to warn a friend about the man she loved. Daisy had advised him to tread lightly with his concerns out of fear of Victoria deciding to marry the guy knowing David had reservations. The last thing he'd wanted was to put any more doubts in her mind when she already had her own.

So he'd kept his mouth shut even as he watched her get more and more involved with Shannon as the last year unfolded. Now that she had, in fact, been hurt by the guy, he wondered if he should've done more to prepare her for that possibility.

He took those concerns to bed with him, where he waited for Daisy to join him. She came in a few minutes later, closing the door behind her.

"How is she?"

"Not great. She's going to watch some TV and try to sleep." Daisy sat on the bed and kicked off her flip-flops. "I feel so bad for her. I can't imagine how hard it must've been to find out what'd happened to Shannon and then to lose him over it." She turned so she could see him. "You saw this coming."

"I didn't see this particular scenario, but you know I've been worried that he wasn't as invested as she is. I should've said something."

"No, I still believe you really shouldn't have. What if, down the road, she ends up married to him? Then you're the friend who doubted the man she loves. Take it from me. I've been the girl in a relationship where everyone in my life hated the guy. With good reason, as it turned out in all instances, but no one could've told me that when I was in it. Love makes people blind."

"Is that so?" He reached for her hand. "What are you blind to when it comes to me?"

"The fact that you're thirty years old and still eating Cap'n Crunch."

David laughed and feigned offense. "I love my Cap'n Crunch."

"I know." She leaned in to kiss him. "And I love you, which is why I buy it for you."

David drew her into bed with him. "What else are you blind to?"

"That sometimes you forget to put the seat down."

"I do not! I was raised with sisters. I know better."

"Once in a blue moon."

"I require proof of this character flaw."

Daisy giggled at his outrage. God, he loved her so damned much. Witnessing Victoria's heartbreak up close made him so thankful for Daisy and the life they had together.

"I'll take a picture next time."

"You do that. Is there anything else?"

"No," she said, smoothing her fingers through his hair.

"Would you tell me if there was?"

"If it was something important. Would you tell me?"

"You'll never be anything other than perfect to me."

She snorted with laughter. "That is such bull. How about last week when I saw a perfectly good chair by the side of the road that I wanted to bring home, and you said we don't need other people's junk?"

"What about it?"

"You don't think my attachment to other people's junk is a character flaw?"

"Not at all. I think it's a throwback to a time in your life when you couldn't afford better. Now you can buy your own junk brand new."

"But why would I waste money on something brand new when there's a perfectly good free version right in front of me that I can clean and paint and make new again?"

"So what you're telling me is you're always going to be a frugal Fannie?"

"Yep, and you're going to have to live with it."

"Most men would say that frugality in no way counts as a character flaw in a potential wife."

She raised a brow. "A *potential* wife?"

"I mean *future* wife. Nothing potential about it."

"That's much better."

David reached up to frame her sweet face with his hands. "I'm extra thankful for you tonight. I wish everyone we love could be as happy as we are."

"I wish that, too, but we worked long and hard to get where we are now. It wasn't always easy."

"Yes, it was."

"Are you remembering the same things I am?"

"I remember every minute of it, and it has always been easy to be with you. It was other things, outside stuff, that made it complicated."

"True."

David dropped one of his hands to her leg, teasing the hem of her sundress, raising it up until his hand cupped one of her ass cheeks.

"Stop," she said, wriggling. "We can't misbehave when our friend is heartbroken in the next room."

"Yes, we can. We just have to be really, really quiet."

"David…"

"Yes, Daisy?"

"We *can't*."

"We absolutely can." In one smooth move, he had the dress over her head and her on the bed under him. Then he reached over to shut off the bedside light. "Shhh." He brought his lips down on hers and knew he had her when her arms curled around his neck.

"We could go one night without, you know," Daisy whispered, her lips pressed against his. He could feel the curve of her smile.

"No, we can't."

"Yes, we can!"

"You're being quiet, remember?"

She poked his ribs, making him gasp and then laugh.

Looking to regain the upper hand, he sat back to remove her panties and bra and get rid of the pajama pants he'd worn to bed. Then he came down on top of her, taking a moment to gaze at her lovely face, visible to him in the nightlight coming from the bathroom.

She looked up at him with big eyes gone soft with love and desire.

"Even after all this time," he whispered, "you still take my breath away."

"Same here," she said in the same whisper. "I love you so much. More every day."

He made slow, sweet love to her, taking his time and reveling in her soft gasps and the quiet moans that he muffled by kissing her. Afterward, he held her in his arms, caressing her back and marveling at her soft skin. "That was so much hotter because we had to be quiet."

"I can't believe you talked me into that when we have a guest."

"I didn't exactly have to twist your arm."

"I'm far too easy where you're concerned."

"No, sweetheart, you're absolutely perfect where I'm concerned."

She kissed his chest and snuggled in closer to him. "She's going to be all right, isn't she?"

"In time." It had taken him a very long time to get over the explosive end to his engagement and to put his guilt over the pain he'd caused Janey in the past. And Daisy had suffered terribly in the violent aftermath of her relationship with Truck Henry. "We know how that works, right?"

"Mmm. All too well."

"We'll take good care of her and get her through it. Try not to worry." He said what Daisy needed to hear, but he too was worried about Victoria. He'd never seen her anything other than upbeat and happy. Her tears had really gotten to him, and he could only hope she'd bounce back from the heartbreak. She'd been such a good friend to him and Daisy that he'd do whatever he could to help her through this.

CHAPTER 8

Shannon unpacked his bag in the small room the company kept on the third floor of the Beachcomber. The room contained only a narrow bed, a dresser and a tiny bathroom, so it took him all of five minutes to empty his bag. At the bottom of the bag, he noticed the envelope he'd put there before he left Ireland, the envelope he hadn't once touched since landing on Gansett.

He withdrew it now and held it in both hands for a full minute before he could bring himself to open it. Inside were the photos of Fiona he had brought with him, for no other reason than he wanted to know he had them if he needed to see them. For an entire year, they had remained in his bag, under the bed he'd shared with Victoria.

In all that time, he'd never once felt the need to retrieve them or to look at them. Realizing how long it had been since he'd seen her face, he felt guilty and sick at heart. He carefully extracted the priceless photographs from the envelope and sucked in a sharp deep breath, as if that could somehow assuage the streak of pain that traveled through him at the sight of her achingly familiar face.

How could he have gone so long without needing to see her? That was proof he'd let this thing with Vic get way out of hand. Fiona, *his* Fiona, deserved so much better from him than a whole year without once looking at her photo. Not that he needed pictures to remember every detail. As he gazed down upon her face with the adorable sprinkling of freckles across her nose and the gorgeous green eyes that had always danced with such mischief, he was flooded with memories. For years after her death, he'd relied upon these images and many others to wipe away the ghastly memories of her violent death.

He'd been haunted by the horror he'd encountered in their cozy flat the night he returned home from work to find her dead. As he ran a finger over the golden curls that fell to below her shoulders, he was transported back in time to those awful first days. A shudder traveled through him, and he shook his head as if that could snap him out of the unwelcome trip down memory lane.

Shannon kissed one of the photos and returned them to the envelope. Then he put it back in his bag and zipped it closed, as if that could keep the memories contained in the past where they belonged.

"I need a drink," he said to the empty, lonely room. In the bathroom, he splashed water on his face and combed his hair. The face gazing back at him in the mirror reminded him far too much of the way he'd looked for a long time after Fiona died—haunted and hollowed, as if someone had cut the very heart of him out of his chest.

The one thing that had helped him then was the same thing that would help him now—Jameson Irish whiskey. He went down the two flights of stairs to the lobby and took a seat at the bar where Chelsea Rose, one of his many new friends on the island, held court most nights.

She came over to greet him with a smile, placing a cocktail napkin on the dark wood in front of him. "How're things?"

"Oh, um, good." Things were a fecking mess, but she didn't want to hear that. She was just doing her job, making conversation.

"What can I get you?"

"Jameson neat, please." He usually drank Guinness here, but tonight he needed something more.

If she was surprised by his drink choice, she didn't let on. "Coming right up." She placed the drink on the napkin. "Are you starting a tab?"

"Yeah. Thanks."

"No problem. Where's Vic tonight?" Chelsea punched information into the computer that acted as the register, so she missed the stricken look that crossed his face, but he caught it in the mirror behind the bar.

"She's…at home." He had no idea where she was, and he hated that.

"Heard she's had a busy couple of days in the baby business."

"Indeed. She's knackered." People would find out soon enough that they'd broken up, but no one would hear it from him.

"Define 'knackered.'"

"You would say wiped out."

"Ahh, I see. We're so lucky to have someone with her skills on the island."

Shannon nodded in agreement and then focused on his drink, hoping to send the message that he wasn't in a chatty mood.

Chelsea moved on to other customers and refilled his glass when he emptied it. She had something friendly to say to everyone who sat at her bar, keeping up a running banter as she served drinks and rang up sales and supported the waitresses and waiters who worked the dinner shift.

Shannon's stomach growled, letting him know he needed more than a liquid dinner or he was going to land on his arse before the night was through. On Chelsea's next pass, he ordered a bowl of New England clam chowder, which had become one of his favorite things to eat since he'd come to Gansett.

He ate the soup and was working on his third glass of Jameson when someone took the seat next to his. Glancing to the right, he saw Dr. Kevin McCarthy lean over the bar to kiss Chelsea. The two of them had been together for months now. He and Vic had hung out with them a couple of times, and Shannon had enjoyed the doctor's company as well as his wise insights on life.

"How's it going?" Kevin asked Shannon when Chelsea went to tend to customers at the other end of the bar.

"Good. You?"

"Never better." As he spoke, Kevin's gaze landed on Chelsea. They were madly in love, or so it seemed to Shannon.

"Glad to hear it."

"You here by yourself?"

"Yep." He didn't offer any explanation, and Kevin didn't ask for one. No time like the present to start getting used to flying solo again.

The two men made small talk as they sipped their drinks and took in the activity around the bar. A solo guitarist, another guy from Ireland named Niall Fitzgerald, added to the atmosphere on the deck that overlooked the ferry landing and South Harbor. Shannon took in the sight of the ferry that would make the first trip off the island tomorrow, a reminder that he wasn't allowed to go to work for the next three days. What the hell would he do with himself for that long without work or Victoria to be with or anything else to do?

He rubbed his chest, hoping the panicky feeling would subside.

"What's the matter with you tonight?" Kevin asked, shocking Shannon out of his ruminations.

"Nothing."

"You're wired and antsy and drinking like a man looking for oblivion."

"Don't shrink me, Doc." The comment came out more harshly than Shannon had intended.

"I'm not. Just commenting on what I'm seeing."

Shannon had no response to that.

"What happened to your hand?" Kevin asked, nodding toward Shannon's bruised and swollen knuckles.

"Got it caught in a door at work."

"Ouch." Kevin took a drink from the beer he'd been nursing for an hour now. "So, hey, I was talking to an old college friend of mine today. He just got back from a trip to Ireland. Said the highlight was Killarney. You ever been there?"

Relieved by the new topic that didn't focus on what was wrong with him, Shannon nodded. "It's down in County Kerry. Nice place."

"You from anywhere near there?"

He shook his head. "My family is from Wicklow on the Irish Sea side. Kerry is on the Atlantic side."

"Ahh, gotcha. I told him I had a friend named Shannon, and he said that's not a very common name for men in Ireland."

"Don't I know it," Shannon said with a grunt of laughter. "It was my mother's maiden name. She thought it would be unique. It's given me more grief than anything."

"Oh, I see. That makes sense."

"Glad it does to you."

"Visiting Ireland is on my bucket list."

"You'll like it."

"I have no doubt I'll love it. You ever get homesick?"

The question hit Shannon squarely in the chest. He hadn't been. "Not really. I like it here." Or he'd liked it here until today, when it all went to shite. *I love you, Shannon. I'm in love with you. I want a life with you. I want us to have so much more than a shared address, a shared bed and the best sex I've ever had. I want a family. I want kids and a husband and a commitment from a man who loves me and only me. I want the fairy tale.*

He couldn't stop seeing her tears or the imploring expression on her lovely face. His Vic didn't cry or beg. His Vic was a joyful, happy person, and he'd reduced her to tears.

"Where'd you go, man?" Kevin asked.

Shannon realized he'd checked out of the conversation. "Sorry, what were you saying?"

"I was just saying how much I like it here, too." As he spoke, Kevin's gaze landed on Chelsea. "Feels like home."

Shannon took a deep breath and exhaled it slowly. Gansett did feel like home, or it had while he was with Vic in their little house. Now, home was a tiny temporary room in a hotel. Goddamn, he'd made a fecking mess of things. He pointed to his glass, asking Chelsea for a refill. Was that his third or fourth? He'd lost count.

Niall took a break and came over to say hello, shaking Shannon's sore hand, which hurt like a bugger, and clapping him on the back. They'd met months ago right here at the Beachcomber, bonding over their shared heritage. Niall's dark brown hair was cut short, and he had big blue eyes that the ladies went nuts over.

"You know Kevin McCarthy?" Shannon asked.

"I do." Niall shook Kevin's hand. "Nice to see you again, Doc."

"Likewise," Kevin said. "Love your music."

"Thanks, mate." To Shannon, Niall said, "Where's Vic tonight?"

The ache in Shannon's chest intensified every time someone asked for her. He supposed he'd have to get used to that. "Taking the night off," Shannon replied as he took a deep slug of whiskey, relishing the burn of it landing in his gut.

Niall visited with them for a few minutes. "I've got something for you in the next set," he said to Shannon before he moved on to greet other friends.

"Nice guy," Kevin said.

"Yeah, he's great. He's a big deal back home. Came here to record with Evan at the studio," Shannon said of Kevin's nephew, Evan McCarthy, who owned Island Breeze Records. "Hoping to break out in the US."

"He's sure got the talent, and with Evan on his side, he'll get there."

A few minutes later, Niall returned to his post on the deck. "Sending this one out to my buddy Shannon and all my fellow Irishmen."

As Niall played the opening notes of "In the Rare Old Times," a song made famous at home by The Dubliners, the pain in Shannon's chest became so intense, he feared he might be having a heart attack. The song had been one of Fiona's favorites, and it brought back a tsunami of memories that, combined with his intake of whiskey, threatened to wreck him.

"Doc," he whispered to Kevin. "I... I need a friend. Get me out of here, will you?"

To his credit, Kevin didn't ask any questions. He signaled to Chelsea to let her know they were leaving.

"My tab..."

"I've got it. No worries."

Shannon didn't have the ability to argue. He'd square up with him later, when he could breathe again.

Kevin took him by the arm and escorted him out of the bar. Thankfully, Niall was engaged with his audience and didn't see them leave. They went out the back way and followed a crushed-shell pathway to a nearby set of stairs. "Go on up," Kevin said.

"What is this place?"

"My office."

Shannon trudged up the stairs and stepped aside to let Kevin unlock the door at the top. He ushered Shannon into the dark space and turned on a light.

"Have a seat."

Shannon landed in the first chair he encountered, dropping his head into his hands. How had it come to this? How had everything fallen apart again so suddenly, the same way it had once before?

"Drink this," Kevin said, handing him a bottle of water.

Shannon opened the bottle and took a drink, letting the cool liquid soothe his parched throat.

Kevin sat in the seat across from him and appeared to wait for him to say something.

Shannon appreciated that Kevin didn't push him, but let him know he was there if Shannon wanted to talk about it. He didn't. Not really, but the pain inside him was unbearable enough that it compelled him to speak.

"I've royally fecked it up with Vic."

"How so?"

"I kept something big from her the whole time we've been together."

"What did you keep from her?"

Shannon kept his gaze trained on the floor, visions of Fiona alive and dead spiraling through his mind like a kaleidoscope of soaring highs and the most crushing of lows.

"Nine years ago," he began haltingly, "my girlfriend, Fiona, was raped and murdered in our flat in Dublin. We'd been together since we were fifteen."

Kevin's deep sigh said it all. "Start at the beginning."

***

Blaine walked baby Adeline from one end of the house to the other, patting her back and putting a gentle bounce in his step the way he'd seen Tiffany do earlier. As she'd practically been asleep on her feet, he'd sent her to bed, assuring her he could handle baby duty for a couple of hours on his own.

He'd never in his life been so intimidated by a seven-pound being who held his heart firmly in the grasp of her tiny hand. She looked up at him with big eyes that couldn't make out much of anything yet, or so Tiffany had told him. But she seemed to be studying him with wisdom well beyond her one day of life.

"I bet you're going to be a genius. One of those exceptional kids who skips grades and graduates early from college."

He laughed at his own silliness and continued to stare down at her, fascinated by every movement of her lips, every expression on her face. Hell, everything she did fascinated him. To think that he and Tiffany had created this new life together was among the most overwhelming things he'd encountered yet in his life.

Sitting on the sofa with his feet on the coffee table and the baby propped on his legs, he was thrilled by the squeeze of her hands around his index fingers.

"The first time I ever saw your mom, I knew she was going to change my life. She was the most beautiful girl I'd ever seen, until I met your sister, Ashleigh, and found out there were two beautiful girls to love. And now there're three of you. That makes me the luckiest guy who ever lived. You know that?"

Her lips made an adorable little bow, and then she blew out spit bubbles that made him laugh. "You'll go easy on your dear old dad, won't you? You should know from the beginning that I'm going to be kind of a pain about boys and all that nonsense. I know what they want, and they aren't getting it from my girls. I'll throw them in jail if they even look at you or your sister."

She did some more gurgling, perhaps in protest of his stance on boys.

"We might be getting a little ahead of ourselves talking about that now, but it's probably best if you know my position on these things from the beginning."

A soft tap on the back door had Blaine collecting the baby and rising to let in his brother-in-law, Mac McCarthy.

"Did you get my text?" Mac asked.

"Nope. Haven't been near my phone all day."

"Ashleigh forgot Boo Boo Blankie when she was here earlier, and there's a bit of a meltdown going on at my house. I told her I'd come get it."

"Oh damn, thank you. She won't sleep without Boo Boo. Let me get it for you." Blaine went up to Ashleigh's room and retrieved the beloved blanket. They'd had to buy a second one for when the original was in the wash. "Are you going to have a blankie, too?" he asked Addie, who stared up at him with those big eyes. He was convinced that she saw him clearly and knew exactly who he was. All the times he'd talked to her through Tiff's belly had paid off. She knew her daddy's voice.

Blaine took the blanket downstairs and handed it over to Mac. "Thanks for coming to get it."

"No need to thank me. We're all looking forward to actually sleeping tonight."

Knowing full well how Ashleigh was about that blanket, Blaine laughed. "At least someone will be sleeping tonight. Little Miss Addie is wide awake."

"How's she doing?" Mac asked, gazing down at her.

"She's great. We've been having a nice little talk about boys and how I'll throw them all in jail if they step out of line."

Mac laughed so hard, he startled the baby. "Sorry."

"Is it always like this?" Blaine asked his longtime friend who was now his brother-in-law, too.

"Like what?"

"So intense that you feel like your nerve endings are on fire or something." He couldn't describe the feelings that were all new to him.

"Nah. You get used to it after a while, and you settle into the new normal."

"That's good, because I don't know if I could handle this much emotion on a daily basis."

"When Maddie had Thomas, one of the ladies she worked with at the hotel gave her a pillow that said motherhood is like having your heart walking around outside your body. If you do it right, and you totally will, fatherhood is like that, too. It's not just about you anymore. It's about something so much bigger than you'll ever be."

"Yeah," Blaine said, gazing down at the tiny face that had become the center of his universe in one momentous day. "That's very true."

"You got this." Mac squeezed his shoulder. "And now I'm off to pacify your other little girl."

"You're the best uncle ever. Thanks for having Ash."

"We love having her. She keeps Thomas and Hailey thoroughly entertained."

"We'll talk to you guys in the morning."

"Try to sleep when she does," Mac said. "That'll be critical for the next couple of months."

"Will do." Blaine saw him out and locked the door behind him. "What should we do now?" he asked Addie. "Want to watch some *Sports Center*? Or maybe *Cops* is on and you can see how Daddy catches the bad guys. Not too many of them on Gansett Island, thankfully. It's more about the fools who don't know when to quit drinking around here."

"What're you telling her?" Tiffany asked as she came downstairs wearing a silk gown that showed off her incredible pregnancy curves. She'd told him they didn't get to keep the much bigger than usual breasts, so he'd enjoy them while he could.

"It's between my daughter and me. No mommies allowed. And why aren't you sleeping?"

Tiffany sat gingerly next to them on the sofa, grimacing from the pain. "Did I hear Mac down here?"

"You did. He came to get Boo Boo Blankie, which Ashleigh left here earlier."

"Oh jeez. How did we let her forget that?"

"A few other things on our minds today."

"How's she doing?" Tiffany asked, leaning in for a closer look at the baby.

"She's doing great. In fact, I think it's possible she might be intellectually advanced."

"And you can tell this how?" she asked dryly.

"She gurgles at all the right times, like she's trying to talk to me."

"I hate to tell you, but that probably means she has gas."

"Don't listen to Mommy. You don't have gas. Daddy knows best, and he says you're a genius." He couldn't stop staring at the baby. "Look at her. Have you ever seen anything more perfect than she is?"

"Only her sister at the same age. She looks just like Ashleigh did."

"I know. I've seen the pictures. I'm going to have two daughters who look just like their hot babe mother. What did I ever do to deserve such a burden?"

Tiffany laughed. "You fell in love with the wrong woman."

"No, baby," he said, stealing a kiss. "I fell in love with the best woman in the whole wide world, and she's made me so much happier than I ever knew I could be."

Tiffany rested her head on his shoulder. "You've made her just as happy."

CHAPTER 9

George Alexander Martinez II had one hell of a set of lungs on him, and he was giving them a full workout as his dad tried to settle him. But nothing Alex did would calm the little guy.

"Come on, buddy. Tell me what you need. Mommy fed you, your diaper is dry and you had a good long nap. What's the problem?"

Unfortunately, little George had no response to his father's query. For the hundredth time since George arrived, Alex lamented that babies didn't come with handbooks that told clueless dads what to do when their wives were off getting some much-needed sleep and they were left in charge of their precious bundle of joy.

"Let's go outside," Alex said. He had no clue whether that was a good idea, but nothing else he'd done had soothed the baby. He'd turned the AC way down, but it was still somewhat chilly in the house—maybe too chilly. Alex stepped out the front door into a warm summer night thick with humidity. Even over the sound of the baby's cries, Alex could hear the crickets and cicadas as well as the belches of frogs, the sounds of summer on Gansett. Overhead, the sky was full of stars, and Alex was reminded of the heat wave during which he'd met Jenny at the lighthouse.

"Did you know your mama threw tomatoes at me the first time we met? Hit me square in the back, too. She's got good aim, your mom. Don't mess with her. That's my advice."

Miraculously, the baby stopped crying. He blinked rapidly, as if trying to process his new environment.

Alex walked along the dirt laneway that led from his house to the house he'd grown up in, where his brother, Paul, now lived with his wife, Hope, and stepson, Ethan. Both their homes were located on the grounds of Martinez Lawn & Garden, the business George Martinez Senior had started more than forty years ago.

Since the baby's arrival, Alex had been missing his parents more acutely than he had since the day he married Jenny. His dad had died of cancer a decade ago, and his mother, who suffered from advanced dementia, was in a long-term-care facility on the mainland. He and Paul hoped to bring her back to the island when the new health care facility their friends Jared and Lizzie James had started opened in the fall. Alex wished he could show off his new son to his parents, that they could be part of his life. It made him unreasonably sad to know that couldn't be.

He hadn't intended to walk over to Paul's, but he ended up there anyway. Hoping he wasn't disturbing the newlyweds, Alex knocked on the front door. Yes, it was weird to knock on the door to the house he'd called home for most of his life, but the house wasn't his anymore, and he tried to respect his brother's privacy.

Paul came to the door wearing only a pair of shorts, his hair standing on end and his face in bad need of a shave. But what stood out more than anything else was the huge smile that never seemed to leave Paul's face now that Hope and Ethan were officially part of their family. "Hey, what's up?"

"Your new nephew wanted to come over for a visit."

"Come in," Paul said, holding the door for Alex.

"I hope we're not bothering you."

"Not at all. Hope is reading with Ethan, and I was watching the Red Sox."

They weren't inside two minutes when George started to cry again.

"He likes it better outside," Alex said. "Let's go out on the porch."

As the brothers settled into the rocking chairs on the porch, Alex was reminded of the night his mother had said awful things to Jenny and she'd come to find him right in this very spot, imploring him to believe that nothing his sick mother said to her could change how she felt about him. It'd taken him a couple of weeks to see the light. Thankfully, Jenny hadn't stopped loving him in that time. They'd also hired Hope to be their mother's nurse, right here in this spot, and now she was married to Paul.

"What're you thinking about over there?" Paul asked.

"All the things that have transpired on this porch."

"Some monumental things, for sure. I always picture Mom out here."

"It was her happy place."

"Remember how we used to tease her about liking it out here because she could keep an eye on her entire kingdom?"

"Yeah," Paul said with a chuckle. "It was true."

"I'm missing them both like crazy," Alex confessed.

Paul nodded in understanding. "Because of baby George's arrival. I felt the same way when Hope and I got married. We're young to have effectively lost both our parents."

"At least we have each other."

"Always. And now we have Jenny, Hope, Ethan and George, too. More to come, probably."

"You holding out on me, brother?" Alex asked.

"Nothing to report yet. Just a *lot* of effort."

Alex grunted with laughter. "Spare me the details."

"I owe you a *lifetime* of details after having to listen to the two of you for months on end."

"Touché." He and Jenny had lived with Paul while their house was being built.

"Mom and Dad would be so pleased by the baby's name. It's such a nice tribute to Dad."

"It was the only boy's name we considered. Helps that the British royal family made George a cool name again."

Paul chuckled. "True."

Ethan burst through the screen door with his mother hot on his heels.

"Don't scare the baby," Hope said.

"I'm not gonna scare him," Ethan said disdainfully. He'd recently turned nine and had been eagerly anticipating the arrival of his new cousin. "Can I hold him?"

"Sure, you can." Alex stood to give Ethan his seat and then carefully transferred George into his arms.

"Support his head because his neck isn't strong enough yet," Hope told her son as she took a couple of photos on her phone. "Tell Jenny I'll text her the pictures."

"I will."

"He's so little," Ethan said, sounding amazed.

"You wouldn't think he was so little if you could hear him cry," Alex said.

"How's Jenny feeling?" Hope asked.

"Sore and tired."

"She'll bounce back in a few days."

Alex's phone buzzed with a text. He retrieved the phone from his pocket to read the message from his wife.

Where have you gone with my son?

Over to Paul's. Be back soon.

My boobs are tingling.

Why does he get to have all the fun?

Six weeks, mister.

Alex groaned. "Does it really take *six weeks* before we can get back in the saddle?"

"You'll be lucky if that's *all* it takes," Hope said.

"She's mean, Paul. Do something about your wife."

Paul snorted with laughter. "You'll survive the famine."

"I'm not sure I will. I've got to take him home to his mom now, Ethan."

"Can I hold him again tomorrow?"

"You sure can."

"Let us know if you guys need anything," Paul said.

"Will do. Talk to you guys in the morning." With the baby on his shoulder, Alex traversed the dirt driveway that connected their two homes. He would be off for the next week, but then he had to get back to work since this was one of the busiest times of year for their landscaping business. When Jenny felt ready to go back to her routine, she planned to take the baby with her to manage the retail store. Somehow, they'd make it all work.

Arriving at the two-story house he'd built mostly himself, Alex went straight upstairs to the master bedroom, where Jenny was propped up in bed, reclining against a pile of pillows. As she held out her arms for the baby, she looked exhausted and overjoyed at the same time.

"Hey there," she said to the baby. "Did Daddy take you on a field trip?"

"Ethan got to hold him for the first time."

"That must've been sweet."

"It was. Hope said she'd text you the pictures. Ethan is thrilled to have another guy in the family."

"Hope and I are outnumbered. We need some more girls around here." She peppered the baby's face with kisses. "How's he been?"

"Fussy. Lots of crying, but funny enough, it stops when we go outside."

"He's a Martinez man. Of course he prefers to be outside. Future landscaper in the making."

"Ha," Alex said with a grunt of laughter. "I hadn't thought of that, but it's true. In the summer growing up, Paul and I would be outside until long after dark. Mom had to call us to come in."

Jenny reached for his hand. "I know you have to be missing them right now."

"Yeah, I am," he said, appreciating how well she knew him. "Having the baby has stirred up a lot of things."

"We'll take him to see your mom as soon as possible."

Even though his mom would be confused by them and the baby, he appreciated that Jenny would make the effort for his sake. "That'd be nice. Thanks. When are your folks coming?"

"This weekend. My dad can stay for a week, but my mom can stay for as long as we need an extra set of hands."

"So she'll be here for eighteen years, then?"

Jenny laughed as she bared her breast for the baby. "Nah. We've got this."

"Are you sure? He's awfully little. What if we screw him up somehow?"

"We're not going to screw him up."

"You promise?"

"I promise, and you know I never break a promise."

Alex watched in amazement as the baby latched on to her breast. "I could watch that all day and never get enough of it."

Wincing, she said, "I'm glad you are entertained."

"It hurts?"

"Kind of, but Vic said that's to be expected for the first week or two, like how your hands hurt every spring until you build up calluses again."

"Not sure how I feel about calluses on your nipples."

Jenny sputtered with laughter. "Stop! You know what I mean."

Alex curled up next to them, putting his arm around Jenny, snug against the baby. "Thank you for giving me a son."

"Thank *you* for giving *me* a son."

"I love you both so much."

"We love you, too. Throwing tomatoes at you was the best thing I ever did."

Smiling up at her, Alex forced himself to relax and enjoy the moment with his two favorite people.

***

After baring his soul to Kevin, Shannon hadn't expected to sleep, but apparently, unburdening oneself was exhausting. He woke to the sound of Kevin's key in the office door, where Shannon had spent the night on the sofa.

Kevin came in holding a tray with two coffees. "Morning."

"Hey." Shannon cleared his throat and sat up, running his fingers through his hair. In the bright light of day, he experienced a pang of embarrassment over the emotional breakdown his friend had witnessed and helped him through. He'd even told Kevin the truth about how he'd hurt his hand.

Kevin handed him one of the coffees. "How're you feeling?"

"Not bad considering how much Jameson was consumed last night, among other things that transpired. Thank you for the coffee—and everything else."

"No problem at all."

"Sure it was," Shannon said with a small smile. "I kept you here until three o'clock in the morning."

"I'm glad I was able to help you."

"You did help. More than you know."

"So what's your plan for today?"

"I'm going to take a shower, get cleaned up and go find Victoria. At the very least, I owe her an explanation for the way I behaved yesterday and for why I haven't been able to fully commit to her."

"What're you hoping to accomplish? Have you decided if you want to get back together with her?"

Shannon drank from the cup of coffee and took a moment to consider his reply. "You've helped me to see that I'm completely in love with her, even if I didn't intend for that to happen when we first got together."

"Love happens when you least expect it. I can certainly attest to that." Kevin leaned forward, arms on knees. "You need to give yourself permission to be happy again, Shannon. What happened to Fiona wasn't your fault. You couldn't have done anything to prevent it. Her death was a senseless, awful tragedy."

"I know, and you're right. I have to stop blaming myself. Even if I had taken a dinner break that night, it might've been too late to stop what happened."

"That's right, or you could've ended up dead yourself."

Shannon stood and folded the blanket Kevin had given him, leaving it on the sofa. He picked the coffee up off the table and extended his sore right hand to Kevin. "Thank you so much. I'll never have the words to adequately thank you."

Kevin carefully shook Shannon's injured hand. "I'm glad I was in the right place at the right time. I'll be hoping for good news about you and Victoria."

"Me, too. I'll call you for an appointment to start regular therapy." Kevin had made the suggestion in the wee hours of the morning, and Shannon had agreed to continue what they'd started.

"I'm here whenever you're ready."

"Thanks again." As he went down the stairs from Kevin's office and walked to the Beachcomber to shower and change, Shannon's stomach ached from more than just the whiskey he'd consumed last night. He was afraid he'd blown it so badly with Vic yesterday that she wouldn't be willing to talk to him today.

He had so much to say to her and could only hope she'd be willing to listen.

Shannon rushed through a shower and shave, and before he left the room, he retrieved the envelope containing Fiona's pictures to take with him. He set off for the clinic, hoping to catch Victoria between patients to ask if he could see her for a minute now or after work. He'd thought about texting her, but had decided this situation called for a personal appearance. Besides, he was suspended from work, so he certainly had the time to go all out to try to win her back.

He walked through the main doors at the clinic right after nine o'clock and encountered David Lawrence standing at the reception desk, speaking with Anna. David did a double take when he saw Shannon.

"David," Shannon said haltingly, "I wondered if I could have a word with Victoria."

"She's not in today."

His stomach fell at that news. "Oh. I guess I'll try her at home, then."

"She's not there either."

"Excuse me." Anna got up and went through the double doors to the treatment area.

Shannon took a deep breath and forced himself to look the other man in the eye, well aware that he was staring down one of Victoria's closest friends. "Do you know where she is?"

"I do."

Shannon understood that he was going to have to go through David to get to her. "Are you going to tell me where she is?"

"Depends on why you want to know."

"I want to make things right with her."

"She's very upset."

"I know. I... I'm sorry to have upset her. All I want is the chance to explain things to her."

"And then?"

"That'll be up to her, I suppose." He held David's steely stare without blinking. "I love her. I want the chance to tell her so."

David blew out a deep breath. "If I tell you what you want to know, you have to assure me that you won't hurt her again."

"It was never my intention to hurt her the first time. I... There are things, in my past, that I've never dealt with the way I should have. I'm taking steps to fix that now, and... I... I just want the chance to talk to her. That's all."

After a long charged moment, David said, "She's at my place. I'm going to warn her you're on your way. It'll be up to her as to whether she'll be there when you arrive."

"I understand. Thank you for being such a good friend to her."

"She is my good friend. I thought you were, too."

"I was. I *am*."

"Then don't make me sorry I helped you."

"I won't. I want to try to make her happy. If she'll let me."

"I would say that's a very big *if*."

Shannon already suspected as much, but hearing David confirm it didn't do much to reassure him. "Thanks again for your help." He turned to get the hell out of there before he lost the courage he'd built up with Kevin during the night. Kevin had helped him see that confronting his demons was the only chance he had to fix his relationship with Victoria and to live an authentic, happy life. Nothing could ever bring Fiona back, but to ruin his life too would only compound the tragedy.

The thought of losing Victoria forever made him panicky. He'd lost Fiona through no fault of his own, and somehow he'd managed to survive that loss. Just barely, but he had survived. If he lost Victoria, that would be completely his fault. He wasn't sure he'd survive that kind of loss a second time.

Straddling his bike, he fired it up and headed for David's apartment on the James estate, determined to do whatever he could to fix the damage he'd done to his relationship with Victoria.

CHAPTER 10

Victoria woke to total silence and a crick in her neck from sleeping on a strange pillow. Judging by the silence, David and Daisy were long gone to work.

Work. She needed to get to work. What the hell time was it anyway?

She looked at her phone and gasped when she saw that it was already after nine. Then she noticed the note David had left her on the table.

Take the day off. We'll cover for you. Hang here for as long as you'd like. I put a key on the counter if you want to go anywhere. Call me later. D

She sagged into the couch, thankful for the day to get herself together. Facing patients with her usual cheerful disposition would've been a huge challenge today. After a minute, she pulled herself off the sofa and went to use the bathroom and the new toothbrush Daisy had left for her.

Coffee. She needed coffee. David had told her to make herself at home, so she did just that, making a cup of coffee in the Keurig. She took it to the small deck outside to enjoy the warm sunshine.

Her phone buzzed with a text from David.

Shannon was just here. After making him work for it, I told him where you are, and he is headed over there. Up to you if you want to be there when he arrives, but he seemed different and said he wants the chance to make things right with you. Call if you need me.

Victoria's heart began to pound—and not from the sudden influx of caffeine. Shannon was on his way over. He wanted to talk. He seemed different.

Hope exploded inside her. Was it possible they weren't over and done with after all? Would he tell her what she needed to hear and commit fully to her, or was he coming to say goodbye?

The phone buzzed with another text from David. *Vic? You saw my message? Just making sure.*

Got it, she replied. *Thank you.*

Hope I did the right thing telling him where to find you.

You did.

Let me know…

I will.

Don't settle for less than you deserve.

I won't. That's what started this whole thing. Too late to turn back now.

He replied with a thumbs-up emoji.

When she took another sip from her coffee, she noticed her hands were shaking ever so slightly. Her entire body vibrated with excitement at knowing she was going to see him and fear over what he might have to tell her. She'd wanted to know more about his past, but was she prepared to fully experience the horror of it?

Probably not, but if that was the way forward toward a future she wanted with him so badly, then she would do whatever it took, even if that meant making his heartbreak her own.

Fifteen minutes later, she heard the bike in the distance and braced herself for his arrival.

Because he wasn't wearing a helmet, she could see his relief when he saw that her car was still in the driveway. He parked behind her car and shut off the bike, gazing up at her on the deck with a look of yearning on his face.

Her heart beat so hard and so fast that she worried she would hyperventilate, and he hadn't even gotten off the bike yet.

Then he was walking across the driveway to the stairs, coming up slowly, almost as if he was gauging his welcome. She noticed a manila envelope tucked under his arm.

"Hi," he said.

"Hi."

"May I?" he asked of the other chair on the small deck.

Victoria nodded.

"Thanks for seeing me." He bent to rest his elbows on his knees and ran his fingers through his hair, a sign that he was nervous about whatever he'd come to tell her. "I'm really sorry about everything that happened yesterday."

"How's your hand?" she asked.

He seemed surprised that she'd asked. Flexing it, he said, "It's killing me, but I suppose I deserve that."

She didn't disagree, so she said nothing about that. "I'm sorry that by talking to Seamus I made you mad and stirred up old crap you'd sooner forget. That wasn't my intention."

"I know, and you didn't do anything wrong. He's become your friend over the last year, and who else would you go to for insight about me if you weren't getting it from me?"

"I would've much rather have gotten it from you."

"I know." After a pause, he said, "What exactly did Seamus tell you about Fiona?"

Realizing his use of her name was a big deal—and a good sign—Victoria said, "Only that you'd been together for years when she was murdered."

Shannon nodded, and after a deep sigh, he began to talk. As always, Victoria was mesmerized by his accent as much as the words he was finally sharing with her. "We met in school when we were fifteen. Her family moved to Wicklow that summer, and she started school with us that year. I was immediately taken with her. We became the best of friends, and then, later, when we were older, much more. Looking back with hindsight, I think I was in love with her from the start."

"What did she look like?"

Shannon handed over the envelope he'd brought.

Victoria's hands trembled as she opened the envelope and carefully removed the priceless photographs of the stunningly beautiful woman he'd loved and lost. Fiona had curly strawberry-blonde hair, blue eyes, fair Irish skin and freckles across her nose and under her eyes. "She was beautiful," Victoria said.

"Aye, she was. Inside and out. You couldn't find a sweeter person anywhere. She never had a bad word to say about anyone and could find the good in even the most difficult people. She'd gotten into modeling and met some truly awful people at various jobs, but she didn't let them get to her. I admired her and tried to be more like her. I dealt with my fair share of idiots as a bartender, and she would tell me there was probably some reason they were that way, and to try to have empathy toward them rather than getting angry."

"She sounds like a saint."

"I wouldn't go that far," he said with a gruff laugh. "She swore like a sailor and could knock back the pints with the best of us. I think you would've liked her."

"I'm sure I would have." Victoria carefully returned the photos to the envelope and handed it back to him. "Thank you for sharing her with me."

"I should've done it a long time ago. Maybe if I had, we wouldn't be in the spot we are now."

"Will you tell me what happened to her?"

Before her eyes, his entire body went tense.

"If you can," she added. "I'd never ask you to talk about it if it's just too hard for you."

"It is hard," he said. "Even after all this time." He looked away from her and seemed to gather his thoughts. "We moved to Dublin when we were twenty-one so she could pursue modeling. I bartended at a local pub five nights a week, including Saturdays. It was walking distance to our flat, so I usually took a dinner break around nine and went home to eat and see Fiona for a little bit. That Saturday, my rugby team came in to celebrate a big win earlier in the day, so I never made it home until after we closed."

Victoria braced herself to hear the rest.

"When I got home, the door was open. Someone had kicked it in. I... I found her, on the floor. She'd been strangled. Later they told me she'd been raped, too."

Victoria wiped away tears and reached for his hand, needing to offer whatever comfort she could. "I'm so sorry."

"Thank you."

"Did they ever catch the person who did it?"

He shook his head. "It's still an open investigation, but the chances of catching him now are slim. We still hope they will, though. She deserves justice for what was done to her. When I think about her final moments..."

Victoria rose and went to him, sitting on his lap and putting her arms around him. "I'm so sorry if my questions to Seamus brought this all up again for you."

"You had no way to know what the answers to your questions would be, love."

"I knew there was something holding you back, and I thought if there was just some way to scale that wall you've put up around your heart that maybe we could make this work somehow."

"You have scaled the wall. You did it a long time ago."

"I... you..."

"I love you, Victoria. How could I not after everything we've had together this last year? Before I came here and found you, I was totally lost. Someone asked me last night if I was homesick for Ireland, and I hadn't been. Not until I thought I'd lost you. That's when I realized that Gansett has become home to me. *You* have become home to me."

Reeling from his words of love, she had to force herself to stay focused. "Yesterday, I told you I loved you, that I'm in love with you, and you walked away from me."

"I know, and I'm so sorry about that. After I left you yesterday, I moved into the Beachcomber and went to the bar to drown my sorrows in a bottle of Jameson.

I ran into Kevin McCarthy and ended up in his office, talking until three in the morning about the many ways I've been fucked up since Fiona died, ways I haven't acknowledged until now."

"How do you mean?"

"For one thing, my plan was to never again become so involved with a woman that losing her would ruin me." He cupped her face in his big hand and ran his thumb over her cheek. "I was doing pretty well with that plan until I came here and met you."

"I want you to know that I believe you when you say you love me."

"I really do."

"But if this isn't what you want—"

He kissed her then, turning her face toward him to capture her lips in a deep, searching kiss full of love and the desire they'd felt for each other since the first night they met. "It's what I want," he whispered against her lips. "*You* are what I want, and I'm sorry I let you think otherwise for even one minute, let alone an entire night. I was completely overwhelmed to realize that in order to keep you I was going to have to tell you about Fiona. I never talk about her or what happened to her. Not ever."

"Maybe you should."

"Kevin has me convinced of it. He's got me starting regular therapy this week. I've never properly processed what happened, and he's made me see that until I do, I can't be what you need or deserve in a partner."

"You can't do that for me."

"I know, love. I'm doing it for me first, but I also hope it'll help to convince you to give me another chance. I want to make you happy. I want to continue to build a life here with you and make a family together. I want it all with you, Vic. If you'll still have me."

She wiped away tears that slid down her cheeks despite her fierce desire to keep her emotions in check. "I want all of that, and I want it with you. I want it so badly."

"But?"

"Just yesterday, you didn't want any of this, and now you do?"

"I wanted it then, too, but I was so wound up about everything from the past coming to the surface and having to confront something I've never dealt with properly. What happened yesterday wasn't about you as much as it was about that. I reacted poorly, and after a very intense evening with Kevin, things are much more clear to me."

Victoria wanted to take what he'd offered and run with it. She wanted that so badly, she fairly ached from wanting it. But the sting of his rejection was too fresh in her mind to leap without careful consideration.

"What're you thinking, love?"

"I need a little time to process all this."

"You can have all the time you need, but I want you to know one very important thing."

"What's that?"

"Any doubts I might've had were about *me*, not you. I've always known how amazing you are and how lucky I am to have met you."

"That's good to hear. It helps."

"I have a suggestion."

His lighthearted tone made her smile. "What's that?"

"I assume you're not working today?"

"You assume correctly. David gave me the day off."

"Since I'm not working either, what do you say we spend this beautiful day together? We could pick up some lunch and go to the beach. We can talk some more about any of this if you want to."

When Victoria had asked for some time, she'd wanted to spend that time alone. But his offer was too good to pass up. "Okay."

"Can you leave your car here and come with me? We'll pick it up later."

"Sure." Swept up in his effortless charm, Victoria was reminded of the night they met and the instant attraction she'd felt toward him. Nothing had changed since that memorable first impression. Even after what'd happened yesterday, he was still her favorite person to be with.

While he waited, she went inside to tidy up the sofa and to wash the mug she'd used. She left David and Daisy a note thanking them for their friendship and their sofa and let them know she'd be back later to get her car. Just in case the day with Shannon didn't go well, she took the key David had left for her and tucked it into her purse.

When she was ready, she locked the door and followed Shannon down the steps to the driveway. Shannon put a helmet on Victoria and fastened the strap. The brush of his fingers against her chin sent off a riot of sensation inside her. That was all it took to make her want him. The first few months they'd been together, she'd assumed their crazy attraction would wane over time, but it had only gotten stronger.

Smiling down at her, he kissed her and then got on the bike. "Hop on and hold on as tight as you can."

"You always say that."

"I always like the way you feel wrapped around me on my bike."

Victoria sighed because she loved him, even more so after hearing about the terrible ordeal he'd suffered through and somehow managed to survive. She had other questions and would get the answers she needed before she decided anything for certain, but she already knew she would give him a chance. How could she not after hearing what he'd been through and in light of the time they'd already spent together?

He'd come looking for her today, shared his pain with her, told her he loved her and that any hesitation he'd had about their relationship was about him and not her. He'd said and done all the right things so far.

For a day that had started off with such despair, things were definitely looking up.

CHAPTER 11

Shannon dropped Victoria at home and then went to the hotel to change and then to the grocery store to pick up lunch. His spirits had risen exponentially after talking to her, and he was more hopeful now that they would find their way back to each other.

Determined to do everything he could to convince her to give him another chance, he bought her favorite salt-and-vinegar chips as well as the chocolate chip cookies from the bakery that he knew she loved. Anything to make her happy, to put the big smile back on her face and to dry the tears that had rattled him because he'd never seen her cry before yesterday.

He hated being the cause of her tears and was determined not to give her another reason to cry over him. Leaving the grocery store, he returned to the house to pick her up for the beach. She had a beach chair that she wore on her back like a backpack and a bag that he strapped to the bike for the short ride to the town beach.

The beach was busy for a weekday, so they walked along the shore a ways to a more deserted portion of sand, where Victoria spread the sheet she had brought. Then she removed the cover-up she'd worn, revealing a skimpy black bikini. Had she worn that one because she knew he loved it? He hoped so.

After they ate the lunch he'd gotten for them, Shannon stretched out on the blanket next to her.

"Will you do my back?" she asked, handing him the sunscreen. She lay face-down, her head propped on her folded arms, her gaze trained on him.

"Happy to." He took his time rubbing in the lotion on her soft skin. "You want me to do your legs, too?"

"Sure."

Shannon continued the sensual massage on the backs of her thighs and calves, noting the way she squirmed occasionally as he touched her. When he was finished, he lay down next to her. "Return the favor?"

"Of course." She gave him the same treatment he'd given her, and by the time she was done, he was hard as a rock.

Shannon ached so badly that he moaned.

Victoria giggled. "Everything all right over there?"

Delighted to hear her laughter, he said, "Are you teasing me?"

"Maybe a little."

He turned on his side, facing her, so she could see what she'd done to him, watching as her gaze traveled from his face to his chest and then his groin, focusing on the huge bulge in his board shorts.

"I did that?"

Shannon scowled playfully at her. "You know you did." He reached for her hand and linked their fingers. "I hated sleeping alone last night."

"I did, too. I've gotten very used to sleeping with you." Glancing up at his face, she said, "Could I ask you something else?"

"Anything you want." Kevin had helped him see that to make it work with Victoria, he had to open himself completely to her.

"Are there other things I should know about you? Things I don't know that I should?"

"No, you know all the big things about my life and my family."

"I didn't know you played rugby."

"Past tense. That's a young fool's game. I'm too old now to take that kind of beating on a regular basis."

"If I hadn't forced the issue, were you ever going to tell me about Fiona?"

"Probably not. Again, not because I didn't trust you with the information, but because it's just so damned hard for me to talk about it."

"I understand."

"I'm going to talk about it, though. I'm going to do the work with Kevin so I can be what you need and deserve in a partner. I want to be the guy who gives you your fairy tale, Vic, and I want to find a better way to deal with it for my own sanity, too."

"It means a lot to me that you'd put yourself through that, in part for me."

"In big part for you. The fear that I had lost you forever was a huge wakeup call for me. I hope you know that."

"Do you ever, when we're together, mistake me for her?"

He stared at her, seeming dumbfounded by the question. "*Never.* Not one time. *Ever.* When we're together, Victoria, there's no one else but you."

"Will you..."

"What, love? Anything..."

"Kiss me?"

"God, Vic, there's nothing I'd rather do." Mindless of where they were, he moved closer to her and put his arms around her, sliding his leg between hers. He gazed at her lovely face for a long moment full of the best kind of anticipation before he laid his lips gently on hers. Shannon watched her eyes close and felt the tremor that went through her when he deepened the kiss, stroking her tongue with his. After a while, he pulled back but only so he wouldn't get carried away, not because he wanted to stop kissing her. "Do you remember the first time we kissed?"

"Of course I do. We didn't stop until we'd done everything."

"Almost everything."

"More than I'd ever done with a guy I'd just met."

"We've been good together from the start." He kissed her again. "If you give me the chance to make you happy, I promise I'll give you everything I've got to give for as long as you want me around."

She released a deep breath. "I'm probably always going to want you around, if for no other reason than I'm addicted to the sound of your voice."

"Ah-ha, now the truth comes out. It's all about the bloody accent for you, isn't it?"

She dissolved into laughter. "Not *all*, but mostly."

He kissed from her lips to her neck, nibbling on her soft skin. "You've got me extremely hot and bothered here."

"You seem to be having the same effect on me."

"Let's take a swim and cool off." He got up and extended a hand to help her. "Don't look at it," he said of his obvious erection. "That only makes it worse."

Victoria laughed at the face he made at her.

In the water, they splashed and played and ended up wrapped up in each other again. As he kissed her, he cupped her breasts under the water and dragged his thumbs over her stiff nipples.

"*Shannon*," she said, sounding as desperate as he felt.

"Is tú grá mo chroí," he whispered in her ear.

"What does that mean?" He'd spoken to her in the words of his homeland before, but she'd never heard that particular phrase.

"'You are the love of my heart' in Irish, or you might call it Gaelic. We call it Irish at home."

"It's lovely. Say it again."

He said it over and over and over again, holding her close to him as he whispered words of love in the language of his home. "I want to be inside you so badly."

She clung to him with her arms around his neck and her legs wrapped around his hips. "I want that, too."

"Should we go home?" Pausing, he said, "No, wait. You said you wanted time, and I shouldn't pressure you—"

She kissed him. "Shannon?"

Dazzled by the way she looked at him, he said, "Yes, Victoria?"

"Take me home."

***

On the short ride, Victoria told herself she was doing the right thing taking him back and deciding to have faith in him. Their brief breakup seemed to have had a profound impact on him, and he'd come back to her with answers to her questions and the words she needed to hear, some of them said in a language and accent that set her blood to racing.

Shannon drove the bike into the driveway and cut the engine, the silence stark after the roar of the bike. He got off and then helped her, removing the helmet with fumbling fingers that she took as a sign of his eagerness. With his hand warm and firm on her lower back, he guided her inside, closing the door and locking it behind him.

When Victoria turned to him, he scooped her up and into his arms, walking toward the bedroom as he kissed her hungrily.

He put her down on the bed and removed his T-shirt as well as the cover-up she'd worn to the beach.

She had a brief moment of worry about getting sand in their bed, but then he kissed her again, and sand became the last thing on her mind.

"This bikini makes me crazy," he said gruffly as he ran his hands over her ribs and up to cup her breasts.

As she looked up at him, another question occurred to her, one that rocked her to the core and one she probably had no right to ask. But it could be the most important question of all.

Apparently, he sensed her withdrawal. "What is it? What's wrong?"

"I have another question, and I'm sort of afraid to ask this one because it's not a fair question but one I still want to ask."

"Whatever it is, you can ask me."

"I wondered if you might ever love me as much as you loved Fiona."

"Ah, Vic," he said on a sigh. "I already do, but it's a different sort of love I feel for you. It's more grown up and mature. Fi and I were so young and stupid and still figuring out life. You and me… We're past all that nonsense, for the most part."

"Are we?"

"Yeah, we are." He gazed down at her, using his fingers to brush the hair back from her face. Then he tipped his head and kissed her neck on his way to her chest. He untied the bikini top and removed it, leaving her breasts bare to his ravenous stare. "You're so damned beautiful. All I could think about last night is how I would bear to live without you, without your smile and your joyfulness. I need that so bad. I need *you*, Vic."

"You have me. I'm here, and I'm going to be here for as long as you need me."

"Forever?"

"That's an awfully long time."

"Won't be long enough." He kissed down the center of her, tugging at her bikini bottoms and helping her out of them.

"Hurry, Shannon," she said, sounding as breathless as she felt. "I want you."

His hair fell over his forehead and his cheeks were flushed the way they got when he was turned on. She loved knowing that about him, and other things, too, like how to arouse him to the point of madness.

Victoria held out her arms to him.

He removed his shorts and came down on top of her. "I wanted to take my time," he said.

She smiled up at him. "We have all day."

"Mmm, I like the sound of that. All day to love you and hold you and kiss you." He entered her in one deep thrust that had her arching into him, wanting to be as close to him as she could get. "Vic…"

Victoria held him tight against her as their bodies moved together in the perfect harmony they'd had since the beginning. "Tell me again, Shannon, in your words."

"*Is tú grá mo chroí,*" he said. "The love of my heart."

She closed her eyes against the burn of tears. "*Is tú grá mo chroí*," she said, tightening her hold on him. "Always."

***

Thank you for reading Victoria and Shannon's story, the first of the new Gansett Island Episodes novella series that will allow me to spend more time on past characters who have additional story to be told or those, such as Victoria and Shannon, who haven't had the spotlight on them yet. I really enjoyed writing this novella, and I hope you loved reading Victoria and Shannon's story and catching up with some of your favorite Gansett Island characters. The next Episode will feature Kevin and Chelsea. I don't yet have a release date for that one, but if you are on my newsletter mailing list at marieforce.com, I will let you know as soon as I have more information.

To chat about this Episode, join the Reader Group at www.facebook.com/groups/GansettEpisodesS1E1/ where spoilers are allowed and encouraged. Keep up with the Gansett Island Series at www.facebook.com/groups/McCarthySeries/.

Many thanks to Team Jack, the ladies who keep me organized and make it possible to write as much as I do: Julie Cupp, Lisa Cafferty, Holly Sullivan, Isabel Sullivan, Nikki Colquhoun, Cheryl Serra, Ashley Lopez and Courtney Lopes. To my crack editorial team of Linda Ingmanson and Joyce Lamb, as well as my beta readers, Anne Woodall and Kara Conrad, I appreciate you all so much. I couldn't imagine releasing a book without all of your eagle eyes on it first.

A special thank-you to Sarah Spate Morrison, Family Nurse Practitioner, for keeping me straight on the medical details in my books.

And to my dear friend Michelle Farrell in Ireland, a huge thank-you for your help in "Irishing up" the dialogue in this novella. A little side story about Michelle… Several years ago, she got in touch to tell me she and her sister, Susan, would be traveling from Ireland to tour New England to see the places I write about. She asked for some recommendations of places to stay in Newport. When

I heard the reason they were coming, I had to meet them! We had a fabulous (and funny) dinner together while they were in Newport, and then Michelle and Susan attended Reader Weekend the following year. Michelle and I have kept in close touch ever since. I was one of the first to hear when she met a new guy named David, who was special from the first time they went out. I've had a front-row view of their wonderful romance and celebrated with Michelle when they got engaged last year. As you read this novella, I will be on my way to Ireland with my husband to attend Michelle and David's wedding—in an actual castle! This will be my first trip to Ireland, and as a Sullivan from Newport, RI, I couldn't be more excited to take this trip of a lifetime with Dan. I'm so honored to be invited to Michelle's wedding and to have made a friend on the other side of the "pond" through my books. I wish Michelle and David, who is a hero right out of a romance novel, the best of everything. I'll post pictures from the wedding and the trip in the McCarthy reader group, on my main page at www.facebook.com/MarieForceAuthor and on Instagram @marieforceauthor.

As always, a special thank-you to my wonderful readers, who have embraced my Gansett Island Series from the beginning. I'm thrilled to hear from so many of you every day that you want more of our magical island. As long as you want more, I'm delighted to continue this series. Much more to come!

xoxo

Marie

OTHER TITLES BY MARIE FORCE

Other Contemporary Romances Available from Marie Force:

The Gansett Island Series

Book 1: Maid for Love

Book 2: Fool for Love

Book 3: Ready for Love

Book 4: Falling for Love

Book 5: Hoping for Love

Book 6: Season for Love

Book 7: Longing for Love

Book 8: Waiting for Love

Book 9: Time for Love

Book 10: Meant for Love

Book 10.5: Chance for Love, *A Gansett Island Novella*

Book 11: Gansett After Dark

Book 12: Kisses After Dark

Book 13: Love After Dark

Book 14: Celebration After Dark

Book 15: Desire After Dark

Book 16: Light After Dark

Gansett Island Episodes, Episode 1: Victoria & Shannon

Book 2: Valorous

Book 3: Victorious

Book 4: Rapturous

Book 5: Ravenous

Book 6: Delirious

Romantic Suspense Novels Available from Marie Force:
The Fatal Series
One Night With You, *A Fatal Series Prequel Novella*

Book 1: Fatal Affair

Book 2: Fatal Justice

Book 3: Fatal Consequences

Book 3.5: Fatal Destiny, *the Wedding Novella*

Book 4: Fatal Flaw

Book 5: Fatal Deception

Book 6: Fatal Mistake

Book 7: Fatal Jeopardy

Book 8: Fatal Scandal

Book 9: Fatal Frenzy

Book 10: Fatal Identity

Book 11: Fatal Threat

Single Title
The Wreck

ABOUT THE AUTHOR

Marie Force is the *New York Times* bestselling author of more than 50 contemporary romances, including the Gansett Island Series, which has sold nearly 3 million books, and the Fatal Series from Harlequin Books, which has sold 1.5 million books. In addition, she is the author of the Butler, Vermont Series, the Green Mountain Series and the erotic romance Quantum Series, written under the slightly modified name of M.S. Force. All together, her books have sold more than 5.5 million copies worldwide!

Her goals in life are simple—to finish raising two happy, healthy, productive young adults, to keep writing books for as long as she possibly can and to never be on a flight that makes the news.

Join Marie's mailing list for news about new books and upcoming appearances in your area. Follow her on Facebook at https://www.facebook.com/MarieForceAuthor, Twitter @marieforce and on Instagram at https://instagram.com/marieforceauthor/. Join one of Marie's many reader groups. Contact Marie at *marie@marieforce.com.*

CPSIA information can be obtained
at www.ICGtesting.com
Printed in the USA
LVHW05s2323180618
581092LV00016B/1429/P